GARY PHILLIPS

Winner of the Chester Himes award

"Gary Phillips is my kind of crime writer."
　　　—Sara Paretsky, author of *Writing in an Age of Silence*

"Honesty, distinctive characters, absurdity and good writing—are here in Phillips's work."
　　　—*The Washington Post*

"Firmly rooted in the hard-boiled tradition."
　　　—*Publishers Weekly*

"And quite frankly it is a rhythm that we don't often hear in crime fiction; the rhythm of black men."
　　　—*BSC Review*

"*The Underbelly* is a swift, hard punch to the gut. An attention getter and definitely meaningful. Phillips is a writer who can keep you nailed to the page."
　　　—Edgar winner John Lutz

". . . a first-rate example of contemporary noir fiction."
　　　—*The Sunday Telegraph*, London

"Gary Phillips writes tough and gritty parables about life and death on the mean streets…"
　　　—Michael Connelly, bestselling author of the Harry Bosch mysteries

PM PRESS OUTSPOKEN AUTHORS SERIES

THE
UNDERBELLY

plus

"But I'm Gonna Put a Cat on You"
Outspoken Interview

GARY PHILLIPS

PM PRESS | 2010

A version of The Underbelly was a first serialized story on
fourstory.org

ISBN: 978-1-60486-206-5
LCCN: 2009912463

PM Press
P.O. Box 23912
Oakland, CA 94623
PMPress.org

Printed in the USA on recycled paper.

Cover: John Yates/Stealworks.com
Inside design: Josh MacPhee/Justseeds.org

CONTENTS

AUTHOR'S INTRODUCTION

When fellow mystery writer Nathan Walpow asked me to try my hand at an online serialized mystery on www.fourstory.org, a site he edits and I now contribute to regularly, I didn't expect that I could complete one in that form—let alone *The Underbelly* would see second life as a printed novella. Imagine . . . print as second life. In just the short span of years since I undertook *The Underbelly*, the traditional publishing world is in something of a freefall. Not to mention the careers of those of us who still love the tactile feel of the printed book in our hands—the hard evidence of our labors at the keyboard.

Kindles, iPads, downloading e-books off the net, reading chapters on your iPhone, social media marketing, it's all in a whirl as ways in which facts and news and entertainment are delivered to readers and viewers. Yet what remains is the human need for order in a chaotic universe, and so our love of stories doesn't cease. Indeed all these, and so many other forms of stimulating certain portions of our brains and hearts, seem to demand more stories, more ways in which narratives tell us of the rise and fall of heroes, scheming dentists and sacrificing single mothers.

Maybe, finally, it'll be a mash-up of you twittering your fifteen minutes of fame via live video streaming and your actions deconstructed by online and cable pundits as part of the never-ending 24/7 news cycle.

Meanwhile, I hope to still have avenues to tell my tales, so much thanks to Nathan, PM Press, and particularly my comrade, the erudite editor Andrea Gibbons, for shepherding *The Underbelly* to print. While I'm down for the aforementioned forms of delivering content, the printed word will always hold the mystery and awe that first gripped me those decades ago as a kid negotiating the aisles of the library at 61st Street Elementary School.

THE UNDERBELLY

"**W**HO YOU SUPPOSED TO BE, old school?" Savoirfaire taunted, flexing his shoulders and shifting his weight onto his
back foot. "Captain America don't live here no more."

"I'm telling you it's through," Magrady repeated calmly,
eyes moving from the man's hands to his face, locking onto the
faux-designer shades the discount desperado wore. "You and
Floyd are done."

"You his father, older brother, somethin' like that?"

"You're missing the point, Flavor Flav," Magrady said. "My
message is what you should be focusing on. Floyd Chambers is
no longer on your loan list. No more vig off his SSI checks."

The two men stood on Wall, smack in the womb of L.A.'s
Skid Row. Unlike the street's more notorious incarnation in
Manhattan, the West Coast version didn't boast of edifices as testa-
ment to giddy capitalism. The bailout around here was of the cheap
whiskey and crack rock variety, the meltdown a daily occurrence.

"Oh, uh-huh." The bottom-feeder nodded his head. "You
lookin' to take over some of my territory, that it? Don't seem to
me like you got enough weight between your legs to be doin'
that, nephew. Don't appear to me you got enough left to run
this block."

Several homeless people had stopped to watch the show.
Both men were about the same height, roughly the same build.
But where Magrady's face was lined and his whiskers grey,

Savoirfaire's decades-younger features were untroubled and un-blemished—the mask of the uncaring sociopath.

"We're done," Magrady said, beginning to step back and away from where the other man stood outside the open door of his Cadillac Escalade. A vehicle with twenty-two-inch gold spinners for rims. Incongruously, Sam Cooke played softly on the vehicle's sound system.

The thug was butter-smooth in whipping out his pruning knife. The blade was vectoring toward Magrady's neck by the time the Vietnam vet reacted, forearm up. The sharp crescent sunk into his sleeved arm.

"What you got to say now, negro?" Savoirfaire gritted his teeth, expecting to easily pull his weapon free while ripping flesh and sinew. But, having been forewarned by Chambers, Magrady had wrapped several layers of cardboard around his arms under his oversized flannel shirt. The knife was stuck.

As Savoirfaire tugged the blade loose, Magrady drove the heel of his work boot into the hoodlum's knee, eliciting a deci-sive crack. The asshole teetered and Magrady landed a straight left to his jaw. He plopped down heavily on the contoured seat of his ostentatious 'Lade, his sunglasses askew. Magrady swiftly slammed the door three times on Savoirfaire's shins, causing him to drop his knife.

Over the yelping, Magrady repeated, "It's done." He then sliced the hook knife into one of the Escalade's expensive sport tires. Magrady walked quickly away as it hissed flat and Savoirfaire screamed profanities but didn't come after the older man. There seemed to be a collective disappointment that ed-died through the small crowd. The dustup over, the aimless now had to return to the crushing dreariness of surviving.

Making sure to move through the back routes, Magrady eventually made his way west on 6th Street. He hadn't been stu-pid enough to expect a rational discussion with the punk, yet had hoped it wouldn't come to violence. But really, why else had Chambers come to him seeking his help? He passed one of the specialty lunch trucks that were the fad these days in trendy ar-eas. This one was called Goro-Ga and featured Korean-style bar-be-que beef tacos and chili dogs made from smoked andouille sausages, and those of other meats including rattlesnake. The truck would twitter when it was coming to a specific location. The aroma surrounding the mobile eatery was intoxicating but the line was too long, so Magrady pushed past. His friend was in the offices of Urban Advocacy near Union at 8th as had been arranged.

"How'd it go?" Floyd Chambers asked cheerily. His strong arms propelled him forward in his ergonomically designed wheelchair with its slanted-in wheels. A residual smell of some pungent marijuana was evident on the disabled man's clothes. Mr. Chambers did enjoy his weed.

"Just peachy."

"Great," Chambers bubbled.

"Cut it out," Janis Bonilla chided. Urban Advocacy's lead community organizer was twenty-eight, medium height, and honey-skinned, with several tats and piercings.

Magrady put his hands up. "It went like it went. You just stay off the Nickel for a few days and that chump's radar and everything's gravy, dig?"

"Don't worry about that," Chambers said. "If things work out like it's lining up, I'm on the ones and twos, homey." He popped a wheelie and spun in a tight circle on the coffee-stained carpet.

Magrady and Bonilla exchanged wan smiles. A month didn't go by when Chambers didn't hint at this or that scheme that was going to earn dividends.

Bonilla's cell chimed "Sambita" by the band Kinky. She answered. "Gotta bounce," she said after a quick back and forth over the phone. "We've got a big turnout happening in City Hall over the Emerald Shoals bullshit. Goddamn gala is in less than two weeks."

"The war goes on," Magrady said dryly.

"The offer's still good, champ," Bonilla said, packing files into her messenger bag. She'd asked him recently to consider being an organizer with UA. He'd been sober this time for eight months going.

"I'll sleep on it."

"Sure you will." To Chambers she added, "See you, Floyd."

"You tellin' it," Chambers replied enthusiastically. The three went their separate ways.

o o o

PAST ONE A.M. IN the flop he'd scored in his army buddy, Red Spencer's garage for the last few weeks, Magrady awoke with the night sweats, his heart thrumming in his ears. He reached for a bottle of whiskey that wasn't there. The jungle had gone hot and yellow in his head again. Booze. Coke. The meds. The group sessions off and on at various VA facilities. All of it had helped and hindered, but none of it stopped the gnawing from returning. He lay on his back on the couch unable to sleep. He clicked on the portable clock-radio nearby and listened to Art Laboe's oldies show.

He once again read through the homemade comic book on stapled and folded lined paper his son Luke had written and drawn when he was ten. It was the tale of Lionhead Mose, a black jet pilot ace who crash-landed in the African jungle, found the secret Ruby Eye stone, and gained super powers. He fought several villains in the thirty-page epic, aided by his sidekick Roy Boy. Magrady, who hadn't seen the comic book in decades, was surprised to find it in the box of stuff he was storing in the garage.

After enjoying the titanic climactic battle Lionhead has atop the Mountain of the Moon against Cobra Fang, he closed his eyes and tried to drift away, suspended between his nightmares and songs by the likes of Thee Midniters and Bloodstone on the radio. An imitation of sleep finally returned as William DeVaughn sang "Just Be Thankful for What You Got."

"I'd be thankful if I had any shit," Magrady mumbled as calmness descended on him and his mind went blank.

Two days later, a black and white jumped the curb in front of Magrady, and the uniform on the passenger side beckoned him over with a motion of his T-handled baton. The cops ferried him to what had been the Greyhound bus station on 5th and Los Angeles Streets. Inside, amongst the luggage and electronic gadget shops, the LAPD had encamped their Skid Row detail. The cops and the denizens called them the Nickel Squad, as 5th bisected Skid Row.

"How you doin', sarge?" Captain Loren Stover had the haunch of his lanky frame resting on an industrial desk, gym-pumped arms folded. His hair had long since departed the top of his head. His office had no windows and the only adornment was a large map of Oregon displaying old bus routes in faded red on one wall.

Irritably Magrady said, "Surely you must have something better to do with your oh-so-valuable time." When he'd last seen Stover, Magrady had been lying on the sidewalk in front of the Watchtower bar. The side of his head was soggy from where it had contacted the concrete after being chucked out of the dive. And there was the captain, all grins and eyes shiny like he was high on the Buddha, the tip of his spit-shined shoes poking the wasted one-time non-com.

The police captain pleasantly asked, "Why'd you do it, sarge, why'd you kill Jeff Curray?"

It took Magrady a beat to realize Curray was Savoirfaire. "I didn't kill him. I defended myself."

"Yeah?" Stover began, getting off his desk. "Well somebody broke his arm in two places, caved in his sternum, then pounded his skull flat like a landing strip at his crib in Ladera Heights. Coroner figures it was a heavy-duty pry bar that some bughouse butthead wielded on the unfortunate." No matter who the deceased was, a pious nun or pederast, Stover referred to those dead by homicide as "unfortunates."

"Bit out of your jurisdiction, isn't it?"

"Savoirfaire had his loan shark and dope hustle on from Inglewood to here. But you're my person of interest." Stover grinned and poked a finger at Magrady. "My theory is after your public altercation, you went away to toast your victory and holed up with some crack ho skank. Sexed up and blitzed out, you got the bright idea you'd better do Curray before he did you."

Magrady was inclined not to argue. What good would it do? He knew Stover was going to remand him to central booking, if for no other reason than because he wouldn't let go of the past.

"When the hell are you going to get over it, Stover?" Magrady said anyway. "It's been so many miserable decades ago, man. We were all just a bunch of scared kids, for God's sake. Kids playing GI Joe."

For a brief moment, glaring at each other, they were transported back to that bubble of time, seconds before that hellacious firefight in that no-name village off the banks of the Drang River. Magrady the green sergeant, Stover the corporal, and his hometown buddy Mike Niles among the other privates in the recon. Mike who Magrady ordered on point that day, and who caught the first VC round, the high-caliber burst turning his brains to spray.

But that flushed away like pissed-out cheap gin as Stover leaned a sneering face into his. "Have a good time in lock-up, sarge. Too bad you screwed up your life and don't have a family or your business partners anymore, huh? Can't hold your liquor. Can't hold onto your woman or the respect of your children."

"Kiss my black ass," Magrady said, getting closer, teeth clenched.

"Don't worry, there'll be plenty where you're going who'll do that for you, honey."

Both breathed hard, each ready to lash out at the other. The door opened. "Get him out of here," Stover seethed to the patrolman, "Get him the hell away from me."

Sixteen hours later, Bonilla arranged for Gordon Walters, a public interest lawyer from Legal Resources and Services of Greater Los Angeles who knew Magrady, to spring him from the Twin Towers jail facility.

"Thanks, Gordy," Magrady said shaking his friend's hand, the large envelope with his possessions tucked under one arm. They stood in front of the facility on the ten acres of the jail grounds, as tatted *vatos* and pretty girls in low-rise jeans with eyeliner on thick as spackle handed out color postcards advertising the various bail bond services located nearby on Cesar Chavez or Vignes to the steady stream of mostly women and children coming in and out for visits.

"So far there is no physical evidence and no eyewitness connecting you to Savoirfaire's murder, but of course the investigation is ongoing," Walters informed Magrady.

"Spoken like a true lawyer."

Walters, a handsome walnut-hued man who stood two inches taller than Magrady smiled. "I'm not suggesting you did it, Em."

"But you wouldn't be surprised if I did."

The lawyer clapped him on his bicep. "I'm supposed to run you over to the UA office. Janis wants to see you."

Walters dropped him off, and Magrady and Bonilla went to lunch.

"Floyd's gone missing," Bonilla said, as she and Magrady shared lunch at the Bent Clock on San Pedro after he'd taken the downtown Dash bus to the location.

"You think he's on the run?" Magrady munched on his couscous. If there was any benefit to the gentrification of downtown, where sweatshops converted to lofts and General Relief recipients and the working poor were being squeezed out, at least the caliber of eateries had improved.

She hunched a shoulder. "The day after your run-in with Savoirfaire, Floyd's Section 8 apartment came through. I reached him on his cell and he was, like, nonchalant."

"Still hinting about his big deal?"

"I guess. Anyway I kinda got angry. We'd managed to help him get the damn voucher in less than two years." They both knew of people waiting more than eight years to obtain the designation considering the obtuse Soviet-style bureaucracy of the housing department. Bonilla added, "So he never came in to get the paperwork, and now his cell is disconnected."

He chewed some more as he considered this. "It's not like Floyd could get the drop on Savoirfaire."

"Because he's in a wheelchair?"

"I know I'm not being all PC and whatnot, Janis, but come on, that mufu wasn't no pushover."

She swallowed some of her smoked salmon and eggs and observed, "A would-be player like Savoirfaire might let his guard down around a handicapped man."

"Stover said Curray's head was bashed in. That would mean he'd have leaned down and let Floyd wail on him."

"He could have sucker-punched him in the gut and when he doubled over, bip," she brought her fist down fast like she was holding a club.

Magrady chided, "Sure, slugger."

The younger woman made a face at him and they chuckled.

After lunch he used Bonilla's cell to make a call, then walked over to the Chesapeake, one of the few remaining Single Room Occupancies in the area. He passed the Weingart Center on San Pedro at 5th Street, a multi-purpose facility serving the homeless. Magrady recalled something he'd read in *Holy Land*, both a memoir and an accounting of how the suburb of Lakewood, about sixteen miles from downtown, was developed. The book was written by its native son, Don Waldie.

Ben Weingart was a Jewish orphan named Weingarten. He was raised by Christian Scientists in the South. He left school in the third grade and would go on to make his money in real estate, helping to build Lakewood along the way.

According to his nurse who also became his lover, Weingart didn't read much save the classifieds to see how his rentals were doing. Where the Center was now had once been a hotel he'd owned called the El Rey which back then had come to be trafficked by prostitutes.

There was hope to be found in that, Magrady reflected. We could all make something out of nothing. After lunch he paid a quarter and took another Dash bus to the Chesapeake. He went up the narrow stairwell to the second-floor landing where the entrance was. A security mesh screen door blocked his way.

Magrady put his eye to the mail slot. Asher, the one-armed desk clerk, looked from the doorway back to the older lady doused in perfume standing next to his desk counter. She wore a thirty-year-old cocktail dress that fit her like she'd just come off the runway.

"No hanky-panky," Asher advised Angie Baine, the one

standing next to his counter. He waved his prosthetic pincers.

"No, baby," the seventy-four-year-old former actress assured him. Her skin was leathery from years of imbibing, but still a kind of haunted glamour radiated from her. "He's here to fix my dresser. You know how handy Magrady is."

Asher made a disagreeing sound in his throat but buzzed Magrady inside. In one of Baine's two tiny rooms, Magrady went through the three cardboard boxes Floyd Chambers had left with her. Among the items, such as a crockpot and the *Best of the O'Jays* CD box set, was a brochure from the archeology department at the University of Southern California and some flavored blunt wrap papers.

"What'd you find?" Baine asked, looking over his shoulder, whiskey fumes palpable. She twisted the cap open on the short dog of Jack and had a healthy sample. Magrady had declined a taste. On the dresser near them, alongside her outdated cell phone, was a glamour shot of the ex-bombshell from nearly fifty years ago. She'd had reasonable parts in two Sam Fuller films, *The Crimson Kimono* and *Shock Corridor*, co-starred in several drive-in second billers in the '60s and early '70s, and even had some guest star work on old shows like *The Big Valley* and the original *Fugitive*.

Magrady held a magnetic swipe card with a familiar logo on it. "You recognize this?" he asked her, indicating the stylized lettering on the mag card.

"Nope. But you can worry about that later, hot stuff." Baine was sitting on the bed, legs crossed, patting the spread.

"There's no time for that now," Magrady pleaded.

"I didn't have to let you in when you called, big daddy." She removed her uppers and winked theatrically.

"Lord have mercy," Magrady grumbled. But he did his duty.

Time passed.

"Why do you care where Floyd's gotten to?" Angie Baine snuggled closer, kissing Magrady on the neck. "You don't plan to turn him over to the fuzz do you?"

He chuckled, kissing her lightly on the lips. "It's not like that, Angie. I just, well, shit, I just don't want to be sitting around waiting for more liver spots to appear."

"I know the feeling."

He took her in his arms and squeezed.

"Damn," she shuddered, reaching a hand down south and clambering on top of him.

Later, the sun almost down, Magrady walked around while he tried to remember where he'd seen the logo on the card. He found himself in front of the sprawling square acreage of the Emerald Shoals extravaganza of engineering, construction and City Hall lobbying. Part of the Shoals fronted Pico at Grand. A good deal of the work was completed, and soon there would be structures including a 75,000-seat stadium where the NFL's Barons would play, moving from the Coliseum in South Central. There was also a fifteen-screen movieplex, a music venue, restaurants and parking structure partially above and below ground.

Two times there'd been temporary halts to the construction.

Once was in its initial phase during some earth moving and digging. Some kind of old pot or some such had been found, Magrady dimly recalled, but he didn't remember what was found—though the eggheads had been crawling around the site after that. The second time was due to the actions of community groups like Urban Advocacy working with public-interest law firms.. The groups had challenged SubbaKhan's convoluted Environmental Impact Report.

That had just been a tactic to get the developer back to the bargaining table to up the percentage of local hires in the community benefits agreement. There was no holding back the tsunami of corporate terra-forming remaking downtown Los Angeles and its environs.

"As Gordon would say," Bonilla had opined to Magrady at lunch, "ride the wave until you crest or wipe out."

"Huh, I'll be," the vet mumbled as he stood before a large electronic billboard fronting one side of the site. The images on it dissolved from one computer-generated artist rendering to another proclaiming the wonders to come, including a music club called the Thrush Lounge and a high-end steak house. In between, the developer's logo flashed. On the card that Magrady was looking at was the stylized SK of SubbaKhan, just like the one that flashed in between the illustrations he was staring at.

How the hell did Floyd Chambers get a hold of the card, and what does it open he wondered. Feeling purposeful, Magrady spent the next day crisscrossing Skid Row and adjacent areas trying to get a bead on Chambers, initially with little luck. He talked with several homeless men and women who, even without permanent roofs over their heads, could be found at regular haunts, down to specific sections of sidewalk on specific street blocks. He finally went to bed that night with a lead, a bar in Inglewood. He slept free of the night sweats.

II

THE NEXT MORNING THERE WAS a tap at the garage door and he opened it to the dour face of his host.

"I'm sorry, Em, but I'm going to need the space back sooner than I figured." Jason Spencer looked past him and tossed the channel lock pliers and screwdriver into his toolbox. Yesterday evening he'd replaced the float valve in the secondary bathroom off the back porch. In the service he'd been a machine gunner in Magrady's squad.

"But I'm paying you, Red. It ain't like I'm freeloading." The sun was barely up as the hands of Magrady's wind-up clock crept past 6:30 a.m. The digital clock part of his clock-radio had stopped functioning some time ago. It was frozen at 3:12 p.m.

"I know, but it's complicated, all right?"

The stocky vet was in his skivvies and ragged T-shirt. The fading letters on it read: *If Paris Hilton Isn't Free, Then None of Us is Free*. Magrady sat on the couch that was his bed in the makeshift living area in his friend's garage. This had been a sweet spot to lay his head, and he had hoped to make it permanent. It damn sure beat having to hustle a bed at a shelter and put up with all manner of knuckleheads and those who direly needed psychiatric care, representing an undertow of the dumped and discarded.

The detached garage allowed him to come and go without bothering the occupants in the main house. There was a mini-fridge, electricity for his clock-radio purchased at the now defunct Sav-On chain, his hot plate and tensor lamp. All this luxury in the rear of a modest Craftsman located on 37th Street east of Budlong, not far from the Coliseum. Magrady still termed this area South Central or South L.A. despite the newspeak promulgated at nearby USC referring to this part of town as "downtown adjacent."

"Like I said, I'm real sorry." Spencer started to walk away but turned back to glare at the man who was once his non-com in a time and place lost to fog and fear square on. "I can't front on you. Fuckin' Stover is the reason. He had Southwest send a black and white by yesterday when you were out," he recalled morosely. Southwest Division of the LAPD covered this neighborhood.

"Said they was gonna give me six kinds of grief for operating a business without a license if they had to come back."

Spencer, nicknamed Red because of his now-greying light brown hair, ran a bootleg body and fender concern out of his back yard. The garage was stocked with pry bars, dent pullers and the like. Spencer certainly didn't make a windfall, but it was enough to keep the widower going, especially since he'd moved in with his elderly mother here on 37th Street.

"Look, you know, if it was just me," Spencer began, making futile gestures with his hand to punctuate his rationalization.

"Fuck it then." Magrady said, the anger he wanted to direct at his comrade not being worth the effort to summon. He wasn't so sure that if the situation was reversed, he wouldn't have done the same. He was back on Stover's radar and the cop was going to work double time to ensure he messed with him every which way he could.

"If it helps, you can store your gear here, okay? I can do that."

Magrady looked at the old fashioned Gladstone suitcase he'd copped years ago at the Goodwill and the small soft-sided equipment bag—the two items of luggage that contained his entire wardrobe. He then regarded the other man and said through tightly held lips, "It does, Red. It does."

He got dressed and was allowed to use the facilities off the back porch before he left.

On the 204 bus on Vermont heading toward the Urban Advocacy offices, Magrady considered where he might stay tonight. Seemed a little early in their renewed canoodling to shack up with Baine, but that would also mean her having to move out of the Chesapeake and he doubted she was so crazy for him she'd do that—both of them on the hustle for a place together. Again, like the old days.

They'd taken up together a couple of times over the years so it'd be best to let their, whatever it was, simmer. Now he probably could bag a couple of nights off of Janis Bonilla, but that just seemed touchy. Not that he'd ever had any, what was the word . . . untoward fantasies about a woman younger than his own estranged daughter. Frankly, he wasn't sure Janis swung that way, as he only had ill-defined inklings about her social life and sexual leanings. Plus, bunking with her would mean she'd be able to needle him about working for her rabble rousing nonprofit.

He figured he could make a go at doing what she did, essentially getting people together, but he'd still have to learn from her. Not that having a woman as his boss bothered him so much as it was a woman a few decades younger than him that stuck in his craw. Damn, he realized, and not for the first time while getting off the bus, he was getting old and set in his ways. To underscore that, his leg favored him with a twinge as he walked along.

"Janis around?" he asked an earnest-looking young man he didn't recognize when he entered the community organization's offices.

The kid stared at him, then answered with, "I'm afraid we don't do shelter vouchers here. I can give you the address of the agency that does."

"Look, man, I'm not—" but he didn't finish it because he was homeless again but he'd be damned if he let this numbnuts know that. "She here or is she off somewhere dealing with SubbaKhan madness?"

That got him a nod. "Yeah, she's meeting with some tenants." He frowned. "So you're in one of her buildings?"

"Would you mind checking her mailbox for me? There should be a check in there." The office used cubby slots to separate their staff's mail. He gave him his name and he went to the copy room where the mail slots were. Magrady nodded to a twenty-something girl with stylish eyeglasses he'd seen at Urban Advocacy events as she walked by. Grace? Amy? What the hell was her name? Shortly the younger man returned with an envelope.

"My bad, man. I didn't know who you were." He pointed a thumb toward the back, adding, "I asked." He handed Magrady his monthly disability check from the VA. Bonilla let her friend get his mail here—what little there was of it.

"No sweat. Thanks, huh?"

"Have you seen your friend Floyd Chambers?"

"No. Fact I've been asking around about him."

"I was the one assigned to help him secure a unit with this Section 8 voucher. And, well, you know he didn't come in for it last week."

Magrady stuck out his hand. "What's your name?"

"Carl. Carl Fjeldstrom. I'm interning here from the public policy program over at UCLA."

"Does Floyd have a brother or sister you tried?" Despite knowing the missing man for more than seven years, Magrady was unfamiliar with much of Chambers' personal history. Such was the closed-book existence many of those down and out maintained.

Fjeldstrom said, "I didn't have an address but there was a number for a sister that I called, but it was disconnected. And I got nothing from Google or information."

"What's her name?"

"Sally, Sally Prescott," he answered after consulting a slim folder he plucked off of a nearby desk. "The number was an Inglewood one," he muttered, re-reading something in the file.

Magrady wondered what else might be in Chambers' file but decided not to push it with the intern. He would ask Bonilla later to have a look. "I'll ask around about her. If the number was funky, then Floyd probably hasn't seen her for a while."

The younger man frowned. "Most of this, and as you can see it isn't much, is from an intake done a few years ago by someone who doesn't work here anymore. I only met with Floyd one time. When I asked him to update his information he took a quick look, said it was cool, and that was that."

Magrady asked, "What changed that you'd get on his case now? I mean, I know they have to keep you busy, but why was Floyd all of a sudden in the running for an apartment?"

"SubbaKhan," Fjeldstrom said tersely.

Magrady waited.

"The fallout from negotiating with them has had a positive ripple effect with some of the other developers along or near the Figueroa Corridor. This particular landlord who has several buildings around here," he indicated the streets beyond the walls, "and near the 'SC campus has been salivating to go condo."

Magrady nodded. The Corridor was the term organizer types used to describe the stretch of Figueroa Street from the northern end where SubbaKhan's Emerald Shoals complex was under construction heading south into the predominantly Latino and black areas where even there, land speculation fever had blossomed. Before and particularly after World War II, South Central had been populated with black migrants from the Southwest and Deep South. Then you could get a house with a down payment from your GI Bill or maybe the check you pulled down working for the city's gas company or the railroad. Magrady, whose folks came from the Mississippi Delta, settled in Chicago, where he grew up running with the Blackstone Rangers.

"What with Emerald Shoals having more bling than this guy can muster, thus already enticing the upscalers he hoped to seduce, he decided it was worth his while to have his buildings remain apartments, and agreed to some low-income set-asides to fill vacancies."

The vet, who consistently had to put up with this sort of inside baseball minutiae from Bonilla, had tuned the sincere young man out without letting on. "I guess Floyd came up in the rotation," he said to prevent Fjeldstrom from going on.

"Exactly."

"Thanks for your time, Carl, I appreciate it," he added quickly.

They shook hands again. He still didn't have a solid lead on a roof for tonight but was juiced trying to figure out where Floyd was and what that had to do with the murder of Jeff Curray, the pissant gangsta who'd gone by the tag Savoirfaire. At the TransPacific Bank on Olympic, Magrady cashed his monthly $719.32 veteran's disability check. Through a pilot program partnered with the bank and Legal Resources and Services, their homeless veterans rep had helped him set up a bank account. He deposited twenty bucks and got some quarters for a five.

Two bus rides and an hour and eighteen minutes later, he walked into the Hornet's Hive on Manchester near Cimarron. Somewhere in the haze that occupied part of his brain, Magrady had the impression he'd been here before, but when was lost to pickled memory. Local radio station KJLH was tuned in over the speakers.

"Gimme a club soda," he requested of the woman bartender. She took an anemic swipe with her rag as he sat before her at the bar. A few patrons, including a pensioner with a metal walking cane, also inhabited the gloomy dive, but none sat together and chatted. The Hornet was where you came to drink and mope and hope for another day. It was also where Savoirfaire was known to conduct his shady business, Magrady had learned.

"Here you go, trooper," she said, placing his glass on a coaster. "That'll be one-fifty."

Magrady forked over a couple of ones and asked, "Any of Savoirfaire's associates roll through here lately?"

The bartender was a dark-skinned, large framed, worldly-looking woman with more muscle on her arms than flab. She wore an Angels baseball cap and pendulum earrings.

"Why?"

His response was a noncommittal shrug. "Need to tighten up with him, you know."

"He something to you?"

Magrady slowly sipped his seltzer. "What difference does that make? We both know he's gone to the happy hunting grounds."

She chuckled. "You don't sound too upset about that."

"Are you?"

The old timer in a worn heavy work shirt with the metal cane leaning against his stool spoke up, clearing phlegm and settled smoke from his voice box. "Hit me like you mean it, Gladys." He shook his glass.

Gladys gave Magrady a put-upon smile, then went to fill the pensioner's order. When she returned she leaned closer, "You don't seem stupid."

Now he chuckled. "Hardheaded maybe." He had more of his fizzy water. "Had a play auntie named Gladys."

"That right?" she said, her smile revealing a tooth with a tiny star-shaped diamond in it.

"Would I kid you?"

"I imagine you might." She adjusted some items below the bar. "Why you so hot to get with any of them fools that ran with Savoirfaire?" And as if on cue, Gladys' eyes shifted from him to the two new clients who entered from the sunlight into the cloying dimness of the bar.

She didn't say anything else to Magrady as her expression told him what time it was.

"Hey now, girl," one of the men said, latching onto the bar. "What up?" He was at least ten years the bartender's junior. His homie sprawled in one of the ancient red leather booths.

"Same old shit," she answered, automatically taking a swipe with her rag in front of him.

Magrady waited until the newcomer placed his order, then pivoted toward him on his stool. The man was dressed in slacks, a colorful shirt and a snap-brim hat.

"Just being curious, but did you inherit Savoirfaire's Escalade?"

The man barely acknowledged Magrady as Gladys returned with his bottled beers. He then nudged his head toward the booth. "Over here," he said.

Magrady followed and sat opposite the two. The second man, in a velour tracksuit, had red eyes complimented by a marijuana fragrance.

"Dude here knew Savoirfaire." The neatly dressed one tipped back some beer.

"Ain't that fascinatin'," his associate slurred, straightening up. He didn't take a sip. He did reach a hand below the table and Magrady then felt the tap of the gun's muzzle against his knee.

"Where's our money, bitch?" Red Eyes demanded, his voice suddenly clear as spring water.

"Let's go outside so you can hear us better," his partner suggested.

On the narrow strip of a parking lot alongside the Hornet's Hive, Red Eyes jabbed the muzzle of his Glock into Magrady's fleshy side. He enjoyed intimidating. "Now what'd you say, old school?"

"I told you I don't know anything about any money that Curray owed you," the vet answered.

"You did say that," Red Eyes' partner offered, adjusting his snap-brim hat. He scanned the boulevard for possible interruptions. An elderly stooped woman trudged by, pulling her groceries in a cart with a bent hub. He stepped into Magrady's orbit.

"Why you sucking around about Savoirfaire?"

"He owes me money too. I've been on the look for him and that's how I wound up here." Magrady gestured a thumb at the outside wall of the bar. On it was a faded and chipped mural of Malcolm X on a motorcycle, Pancho Villa casually holding an AK, and Selena dressed like Wonder Woman. Villa was on a horse and Selena on what looked to be flying disk. The three were side by side on a hill. There was no graffiti sprayed on the images.

"Why the fuck would somebody like the Sav owe an old punk-ass like you money?" Red Eyes snickered as he looked Magrady up and down and glared at his face. "You're bullshit-tin'." To emphasize his point, he jammed the gun in Magrady's stomach, causing him to grimace.

Red Eyes taunted, "Don't like it in the belly, huh?"

Magrady remained silent, assessing if he had any options.

"Who are you?" the calmer one in the hat and print shirt said.

"I told you."

"You told us what you wanted to, but that's not what I asked."

"That's right, pops, it ain't." Red Eyes made to punch him in the gut again with the business end of the pistol and Magrady grabbed his arm with both hands. He twisted that arm and pivoted his hip into the other man's side. Magrady hoped his reflexes remembered those long-ago judo lessons he'd taken during basic. Damned if he didn't flip his tormentor over his shoulder and slam his butt onto the asphalt.

"Mothahfuckah," the downed man swore.

Still holding onto that arm. Magrady placed his foot into Red Eyes' armpit and turned his wrist viciously. The gun came loose.

"I'm impressed," the second hood said genuinely. He drove a fist into Magrady's already tender stomach and followed that with a clip to the jaw that was brutally effective.

Magrady teetered and tried to keep his feet under him, figuring he was in for a boxing lesson. Only Red Eyes wasn't through. He picked up his gun and backhanded it across Magrady's face. The older man fell against the fender of a Volkswagen, and slid down against the car's tire well. The two now towered over him.

"You better stay away from 'round here and don't be nose'n into our bid'ness," the one in the hat stated. "I don't know what the hell you're sniffing around for, but this shit don't concern you, understand?"

"Yeah," Magrady said.

"I said do you understand?" he repeated forcefully, but in an even tone. Through all of this, he hadn't spoken above a normal tone.

"Yes," the beaten man repeated.

"Good for you." Red Eyes kicked him in the thigh and the two left in a dark blue Scion. Rather than rap blaring from its speakers, country and western music pumped from the vehicle as they drove off.

Magrady sat up and recuperated, breathing heavily through his mouth for several minutes. A decades-old Ford pickup with a bed-over toolbox pulled into the lot. The driver, in matching plaster-smeared khakis and shirt, took a long look at him, then went into the bar. Minutes passed. Having gathered himself,

Magrady got up and limped back into the Hornet's Hive. Gladys, the bartender, took in his appearance and produced a plastic first aid kit from below the bar.

"Thanks," Magrady said. He took the kit and went into the men's room. He returned shortly thereafter having mostly applied Mercurochrome to the open wound where Red Eyes had slapped him with the gat. He took a position on a stool, sliding the kit back across the bar top. At the far end was the plasterer, leisurely having himself a martini, ignoring Magrady and everyone else as he munched on an olive. Magrady leaned his elbows on the wood and fought back the urge to order a shot.

"Who were those lovely fellows?"

Gladys frowned as if he were sticking his tongue out at her.

"Names can't hurt, can they?"

"Right," she said warily. "You're an example of that." She went off to fill an order, then returned. "Why you knocking yourself out like this?"

"I hate to be told what to do."

"Who doesn't?"

"Then think of me as Tom Joad, standing in for all who have been put down and put upon."

"You're fuckin' funny." Her big earrings tinkled like chimes as she chuckled.

"I'm all about the charm."

She spritzed him a glass of soda water. "The sharpie goes by Elmore."

"You're kidding."

"No. His mama was a big blues fan. The other one, the weed head, is called Boo for Boo Boo."

"Like Yogi the Bear's little buddy?"

She continued, "Only of course nobody calls him that unless they want him to go straight playground."

"What's his real name?"

"Don't know. But Elmore's family name is Jinks. Not short for Jenkins."

Magrady nodded and asked, "How about a guy in a wheelchair?" He described his missing friend Floyd Chambers.

"Nope, sorry." The Manhattans sang "'Kiss and Say Goodbye'" on the radio piping into the speakers up high in the corner behind the bar.

It was getting on in the afternoon. Sitting there at the bar, gazing into a swirl of dust motes in a cone of slanting light, the effects of the beatdown were overtaking Magrady. Here he was close to needing a walker playing Super Shaft, and for what? Get his head busted open over bullshit, he glumly concluded.

Still, the notion that he could do this, be of some worth, was what had set him going. And too, maybe he'd get one up on that self-righteous prick Stover—surely that was a good thing.

Magrady produced a wan smile and touched his tender face. Unlike the world-weary PI, he had no Girl Friday to patch him up, let alone a place to sleep tonight. Gladys presented possibilities but she definitely wasn't the kind of woman to take a dude like Magrady home on the first meeting. Especially as he was messing with Elmore and the Boo Boo, surely she wouldn't want that kind of grief on her doorstep.

Was his resistance to calling Janis Bonilla just because she'd bug him to come to work for Urban Advocacy? Or was it that he didn't want to appear weak and needy to her? Intellectually he knew she wasn't the judgmental type, so why did he want to maintain certain perceptions with her? Did he dig her in that way or hey, if he was a father figure to her, that too was a reason to show no cracks.

Reassessing his earlier decision, he could press matters and try and bunk with Angie Baine, as getting past Asher the deskman was more of a game than obstacle—at least for a few nights. But it could be a signal to her they were taking up again. The last time they'd tried playing house a decade ago, she'd gone off during an argument, bolstered by the afternoon vodka tonics she imbibed in those days. Going on about how he was devious like this producer who'd screwed her out of her comeback role. She'd nearly scaled the skin off his back by chucking a pot of boiling rice at him. For an old girl originally from a staid blue-veined family in Bridgeport, Connecticut, she had plenty hood rat in her, Magrady reflected. It made for interesting encounters, and she did seem calmer now—but he'd already been roughed over once today.

"Aw, hell," he mumbled. He was too worn out to be scuffling on the streets tonight. "Can I borrow your phone?" he asked Gladys. "It's local, I swear. I mean it's 323." Inglewood was in the 310 area code. A working pay phone, particularly in this part of town east of the airport was rarer than Lindsay Lohan not crashing a car.

Gladys placed an old rotary job on the bar. "Two bucks and you only get a minute. And I see what number you dial."

What had he been smoking? A tough broad like her give him a place to lay his head? Even in the storeroom in this joint? She'd have laughed herself sick if he'd have asked. He paid the freight.

"Janis," he said when he got her on her cell phone, "You give a veteran's discount, don't you?"

"You're not trying to proposition me, are you, Magrady?" she joked.

He explained his situation. Aware, too, that while he was consciously keeping his voice down, the whiskered gent with the metal cane was giving him a couple of glances.

"That's not a problem. Only I'm not getting home till around ten or so tonight," Bonilla said. "I've got a strategy meeting with the coalition. What don't you come by that and then we go from there?" She told him where the meeting would be.

He said he would and ended the call. Magrady thanked Gladys again and got off the stool to leave. His body was stiff and he seriously considered just one brace of whiskey before he got back out there. He could handle that. He wasn't no kid, he was a grown-ass man, wasn't he? Sheeet.

"You were in Vietnam?" The old fella with the cane asked him. He was looking straight ahead across the width of the bar at the assortment of bottles on their shelves.

"I was."

"Chosin," the regular answered. "Heard of it?"

"Sure. It was a meat grinder during the Korean War."

"Blood froze before it could spit out your body," the old man said hollowly, looking off and shaking his head slowly. "We swabbed our M-1s in antifreeze-soaked rags to keep them from freezing up. Toes and fingers getting black from the gangrene 'cause of creeping frostbite." He stopped talking and had more of his drink. He didn't continue so Magrady figured the VFWer just wanted to connect to another GI who might understand what it was still chasing him all these years later. He started to leave.

"Knew your boy Floyd," the other man said. "Knew him before the accident that put him in that chair."

Magrady said, "How'd you know him?"

The other man shook the ice in his now empty glass like a shaman preparing to roll the bones. Or seeking tribute.

Why not? He bought him another round. "Well?"

"Some kind of fall or some such put him in that chair. One of them construction jobs over there in El Segundo 'bout ten, eleven years ago. He was a welder."

"You still haven't said how you know Floyd."

"More it was his sister I knew. Had a little appliance store not too far from here and she clerked there for me. Floyd would come by when she was through to pick her up. She was a looker."

"Sister got a name?"

The other man laughed and it echoed into the glass at his lips. "Want to make sure you're getting your money's worth, huh?"

Magrady remained quiet.

"Sally Chambers."

"Not Prescott?"

"Not when I knew her."

"Since she worked for you, any idea where she lived?"

He completed a leisurely sip, then, "My store survived the Negroes and Mex-cans tearing shit up in '92 only to have some sweet ol' sister on her way home from church suddenly get the Holy Ghost behind the wheel. She plowed that bad boy through the front of my shop like them hurricanes leveled the Ninth Ward.

"Between the hassles with the insurance company and the surviving family of that psalm-singer who went to see the Lord, I said, enough of this mess." He got quiet and simply sat and stared.

"So, could be you have an old file somewhere with her last known address?"

He raised both eyebrows signaling "Who knows?"

"Maybe I can call you down here in a couple of days if you get a chance to look." He handed a five to Gladys. "Another one on me." He needed an expense account.

Rising from his stool again, Magrady asked, "So what made you all chatty?" Long shadows of late afternoon spilled under the bar's curtained threshold.

"You got in the face of those two no-dicks," the old man said, smiling thinly. "Always in here buying a beer for us peasants or haw-hawing about what big men they are. Shit," he drawled. "I survived the goddamn Chosin goddamn Reservoir Campaign."

"Mulgrew Magrady," he said, sticking out his hand.

The other one returned the handshake and said, "Sanford, Gene, but they call me Freddy on account of the old TV show with Redd Foxx." Gladys delivered his drink. "But I'll tell you this too. Now I heard this later, after my shop was gone and him in his chair, she had some kind of situation with her husband then, the Prescott you mentioned. Worked with Floyd he did."

"Situation?"

The old man was sipping his drink and paused. "He got hisself on the slab. I know that."

"Accident? The same one that crippled Floyd?"

Sanford hunched his boney shoulders. "If you think having a carving knife sticking out of your chest is an accident."

"Sally do that?"

The old man regarded Magrady. "He was found in the apartment of this fairy he was bungholing on the side. The sweet boy had an alibi, he was at his sick mom's. And even though John Law questioned her, Sally wasn't charged." Sanford continued his drinking.

"I appreciate this." Magrady left. At a Dawn to Mid-Nite, a cut-rate version of 7-Eleven, Magrady bought and microwaved a chicken and jalapeno burrito. He ate that and drank a grape-flavored Gatorade as he waited at the bus stop. As evening came on, he arrived at the meeting of the coalition of community groups doing work around gentrification. It was being held in a Lutheran church on Figueroa, three blocks north of the USC campus.

"Prone out," a voice yelled from the darkness as Magrady ascended the church steps.

A police chopper thundered overhead and suddenly he was back in 'Nam, back on the LZ as the mortar rounds exploded in his ears.

Disoriented, Magrady's reality tilted sideways then spun corkscrew fashion into a tornado of sensations. In a distant part of him he knew he was face down on the landing of the church, and that several officers were rushing past him. Some not minding in the least that their thick-soled sure-grip Oxfords stepped on his hands and arms. But the main show was given over to the flashes of gore and death making him nauseous and the booming that kept him off kilter.

The flashback fully descended on him at the thunderous whoop and stab of the overhead light of the swooping police helicopter. Magrady didn't try to move or speak. As far as he could tell, there was no officer standing over him with their nine or Monadnock T-handled nightstick cocked to rat-a-tattat the rhythm of compliance on his skull, but he was immobilized nonetheless.

The war's replay uncoiled and Magrady relived, yet again, a soldier named Edwards die spectacularly before him. His entrails splattered over the sergeant's torso as he sought to get his men together for evac on the Hueys while simultaneously seeking to isolate the source of the incoming VC fire.

Breathing like a labored steam engine and his heart lodged his throat, Magrady heard in real time cops and civilians yelling at each other as pews were upset, their wood splintering and objects crashing and shattering on the earthen tiles of the church. Magrady had once gotten a sweet little gig to replace those tiles in a rear portion of the sanctuary due to damage from a broken toilet pipe. He rolled over on his back, his chest finally rising and falling at a more normal rate.

A female cop's face slid into view over him. She was handsome and alert in a stressed out kind of way, and blinked hard at him.

"Is he one of those Sudanites? A village elder or something?" she incorrectly asked someone out of his line of sight, pointing at him. "They're coming over here now, right? All that shit that's going on over there in their desert villages."

A heavy man's voice sighed. "That's one of ours, Reynolds. He's an American black. We can't give him back." The man chuckled. How right he was. Where indeed would Magrady go if he was kicked out of the U.S.? Or put on a boxcar with other malcontents and shipped out of town on a rail, the method of forced relocation practiced at various times on hobos and union agitators in the '30s by the cops and goon squads in the pocket of the big bosses.

He hummed "Joe Hill" as he'd heard Paul Robeson singing it on the 78 platter his mother used to play when he was a kid. Another round of shouting started up, only this was orders given from command to the grunts. The flashback wore itself out and some gendarmes roughly got Magrady on his feet. He, along with the other members and staff of several community-based organizations, were culled together on the lawn of the raided Lutheran church.

"The fuck, man?" Janis Bonilla demanded of the cops en masse. "We don't need a permit to be on private property. We're going to sue the shit out of your donut-eatin' asses."

"Take a chill pill, Ms. Bonilla." A stout LAPD captain addressed her, separating himself from the grouping of cops but not actually moving closer to her. "This was about the illegals at this meeting."

Bonilla and several others glared at him openmouthed.

Armed men and women emerged from inside and around the corner of the building. Stenciled on the back of the new arrivals' jackets was the word ICE in big yellow cap letters, the Immigration and Customs Enforcement arm of the Department of Homeland Security. Accompanying them were unfortunates in plastic restraints—members of the assembled community organizations.

"This is bullshit," somebody said, and there was loud agreement from the gathered. It was the young woman with the glasses Magrady had seen at the UA offices. Amy, that was her name.

The captain smiled knowingly. "This is a new day of joint cooperation. If it bothers you, take your concerns up with your do-nothings in Congress." He walked off.

Bonilla muttered "tea bagger," and began making calls.

III

HOURS LATER BONILLA STILL SEETHED, swirling diet soda in a can. The police and ICE had departed with their undocumented arrestees along with four citizens detained on charges ranging from a bench warrant on a jaywalking beef to overdue child support payments. Naturally the community groups held an emergency meeting after the round up. There would be a formal response involving public interest allies like Legal Resources and Services, and a press conference at UA's offices was planned for the next morning at 10 a.m.—in time to be broadcast on the afternoon news. Already, an e-blast had gone out to political and advocacy blogs about the action, and buzz was building.

"You gonna mention SubbaKhan tomorrow?" Magrady asked.

"I should," she answered, taking a long pull on her drink.

It was already past one in the morning. "But yeah, I know that would be irresponsible, wouldn't it?" Bonilla had already had this discussion with her executive director. There was, at this moment, no evidence indicating the blitzkrieg originated within the Stygian inner sanctum of the all-consuming kraken that as far as Bonilla was concerned, was headed by the tentacled triumvirate of Dick Cheney, William Kristol, and the truly scary eviscerating automaton, Ann Coulter.

"Plus you'd get fired," Magrady offered. "You'd be breaking the detente. Y'all gotta be lining up for your free drinks at the Emerald Shoals opening like the other community partners and unions."

"But it can't just be coincidence," she insisted, glaring at him.

"Look, my boy Stover could have alerted his buddies to keep their antennas tuned to your doings."

She said, "He does have a fierce hard-on about you, that's for sure. I mean, it wasn't your fault about what went down in 'Nam."

"There's that," he said, gesturing with his hand in an effort to halt her from going into painful history. One service-related and guilt-wracked visit to the past was all he could take for an evening. "The other thing to consider is that you have a snitch in your midst."

"What, like a police spy? Like back in the day of Chief Gates and his Public Disorder Intelligence Division?"

PDID undercover cops had infiltrated community groups as agent provocateurs. Bonilla was a student of L.A.'s activist archives. She'd spent hours reading through such files and articles from the '70s and '80s down at a place in South Central called the Southern California Library for Social Studies and Research, a repository of that kind of material. Magrady had accompanied her on more than one outing there to read through old papers from such now defunct groups like the Coalition Against Police Abuse, CAPA.

"I was wondering if it wasn't some turncoat secretly on the payroll of your arch enemies," he opined.

Bonilla didn't say anything.

"Maybe I'm being paranoid, but if I were the head of SubbaKhan, kicked back at my desk puffing on my Arturo Fuente maduro, I'd be figuring out how to stay one step ahead of you Hugo Chavez-quotin' subversives."

"That would be illegal," she remarked.

"I'm not sure it is. And even if that were so, how would you prove it?"

"It worries me the way your mind works."

He smiled broadly. "Me, too."

Bonilla, who'd been pacing, sat down. They were in the small kitchen of her apartment in a 1920s-era building, replete with Zig-Zag Moderne touches on the façade. It was situated on Catalina in a blended area of Koreatown and Pico-Union. Where one could spot *carnicerías* with life-sized plastic bulls on their roofs next door to Korean wedding gown shops, whose display windows contained ice beauty mannequins with thousand mile stares looking out past the neon Hangul onto the changing city.

"That would be some shady shit, ya know?" Bonilla stated.

"I ain't saying you gotta go all black-ops and start waterboardin' fools to talk, but you do have low-income and poor folk you're working with."

"That's bourgeois thinking, Magrady," she groused. "I'll have to send your monkey ass to the re-education camp."

He chuckled. "Or am I being the real Stalinist here? You got people who are barely getting by, Janis. Maybe they have a medical condition or their kid is in trouble with the law yet again. It's not hard to find out who has what problems. If it's legal entanglement, a lot of that's public records, right?

"So one day a swell-dressed man or, better yet, smart-looking woman shows up on my dilapidated doorstep and says 'Hey, we're not asking you to be a sell out or anything like that.'"

"Oh, no," Bonilla snarked.

He continued in character. "We're not asking you to put the finger on anyone, but just let us know, you know, in a general way what they say at those meetings you go to. Now don't draw attention to yourself, don't be asking a bunch of questions." Magrady spread his arms wide and slumped in his seat. "Sit and listen and every now and then we'll call to ask a few harmless questions and in exchange, a few hundreds in nice, crisp twenties will find their way into your house fund or maybe junior gets community service rather than jail."

"Then why bust us for our undocumented members? If I was a spy, I'd want to wait until I had something more juicy."

He wiggled his fingers on both hands. "One branch doesn't know what the other is up to. If the spy is on the private ticket, there wouldn't necessarily be coordination with the po-po. Anyway, this is just early morning after we got our ass kicked speculation. Like I said, y'all are easily targets of opportunity, or this went down simply because those self-absorbed, Lhasa Apso-owning loft-dwellers you despise have been complaining, and this is how the cops respond."

Bonilla rubbed the back of her neck. "We have been trying to recruit some of those latte liberals as allies. It's not like they shouldn't have a place to live. But they also can't act like their shit, and that of their boutique pooches, don't stink. Their attitude is it's them bringing up the neighborhood while the poor get booted out."

"How's that working out? Getting them to see you have some common interests?"

"Don't be cute. It doesn't suit you."

"I take your point, *subcomandante*."

She was reflective, then. "You think that's what Floyd was doing? Why he was hinting about how he was about to get over?"

"Except it seems he had the goods on someone, doesn't it? And there is that SubbaKhan magnetic swipe card he had."

Bonilla pointed at Magrady. "He saw the CEO try to rape this woman. She resisted and when they fought, he accidentally bashed her head in and Floyd, who'd been hired on a disabled program, was in the office late and decided to blackmail the dude."

"Amusing. I saw that movie too. Only that guy was a professional thief."

"Just trying to be as devious as you are, champ. So what if Floyd stole that card from a SubbaKhan employee?"

"Could be. Of course that raises the question of where the hell Floyd could have been with the employee."

"You're the one playing peeper."

Magrady grunted. "Playing is right." He yawned. "I keep getting vamped on but no further along in figuring this out."

She yawned and playfully slapped his knee. "The case is young yet, you'll get onto something."

He stood and stretched, "Yeah, blisters on my feet from hoofing it all over Creation and a couple of knots upside my head."

"Tough guy." She also stood and nodded toward her front room and the couch where she'd given him a blanket and a pillow. "You gonna be okay?"

"This is great, Janis, I really appreciate it." He touched her shoulder.

She covered his hand with hers and let it linger. "I told you it wasn't a problem. I'll ask around if anyone knows of someplace for you to rent out like a room or something."

"Cool."

"Good night," she said, kissing him on the cheek. He flushed and was glad she couldn't tell. At least he hoped she couldn't tell. Damn young women.

He slept unperturbed, as if wrapped in a cocoon of black velour and awoke to the smell of coffee. For the briefest of moments, he allowed himself to fantasize he was back in his house with his wife and children as they got ready for school. But to believe such was cruel and a lie, and certainly not therapeutic. For he'd also have to remember why he'd derailed the Father Knows Best bit with the drinking and the drugs and the erratic behavior, and why it was he didn't have a home any more or any communication with his distanced family. Why maybe he didn't deserve to have those or any such comforts.

"Hey," Bonilla said as they shared coffee at the kitchen table, "Carl texted me a message about Floyd's sister."

"When?"

"'Round seven." It was now 7:40 a.m. "He had to be in early to help prep for the press conference."

"Y'all work your interns worse than green recruits," Magrady commented. He'd asked his friend to ask the intern he'd encountered at Urban Advocacy to see if there was any other pertinent information in the thin file they had on Floyd Chambers.

"Wait, when did you send him your message?"

"On our way home. Carl's a video game fiend so I knew he'd be up killing aliens with his geek buddies online plugged in from who knows where. He lives on those energy drinks."

Magrady suppressed a shudder. "Can you let a brother know?"

She told him and he was somewhat surprised it wasn't an Inglewood address. It was in Altadena in the San Gabriel Valley. He didn't know how many bus transfers that was, though he knew the Metro Rail's Gold Line could take him to Pasadena at least.

Maybe he ought to invest in a motorcycle. But the old TV ad of the elderly lady on the floor saying "I've fallen and can't get up" occurred to him. Where even the remote clapper—"clap on, clap off"—wouldn't be able to levitate him to a seat. This and the number of careening SUVs that populated Southland roadways dissuaded him from getting his brittle butt back on a bike after some thirty years.

"Before we get on our respective horses, Carl had mentioned someone who used to work at UA had taken the information for Floyd's file. Do you know who that was?"

"Sure," Bonilla answered, "that was Shane."

"Alan Ladd?"

"Shane Redding, a woman. In fact she's a paralegal over at Legal Resources now. I'll hook you up."

A little past nine, Magrady talked with Redding on the phone after Bonilla had left her a message vouching for him.

"Sure I know who she is," Redding said after he'd asked her about the sister. "We helped her on a tenant-landlord matter not too long ago. She came to us because we've stayed in touch." She paused. "Because you know Janis, I could try and contact her for you."

"She's in Altadena?"

"No, here in L.A. last I knew"

"I'd appreciate anything you can do on this," Magrady said.

Redding agreed to let Janis Bonilla know if she connected with the sister. Problem was that also meant she would know he was looking for her brother and she could tip him to stay hid. If he was hiding, and if she had any part in helping him do so. That's why he didn't ask Redding if she knew anything about the sister's dead husband. No sense having her mention this to the sister and possibly drive her away. Still he was worried that all this was nothing but the unhinged view of a man in search of a mission when really his best years, if he had any, were behind him.

Sitting in the tidy breakfast nook of the organizer's apartment, enjoying his morning coffee in stoneware instead of Styrofoam, it occurred to Magrady maybe Bonilla was just humoring him. Sharp young chicks like her knew the best way to handle addled oldsters like his rootless self. She dealt with all sorts of barely hanging on tenants, folk who should be receiving outpatient psychiatric services or would do better institutionalized.

He'd watched her soothing the agitated without being condescending. She'd coax their stories of neglect and mistreatment out of them with the precision patience of a *mohel* about to do the cut in a bouncing rickshaw. Dealing with individuals who kidded themselves they were okay and went off their meds or who'd been booted or fallen out of the system due to the infinite and unknowing regulations of the great and grand bureaucracy. Bonilla working herself raw to cobble together a membership of undocumented busboys and brothers Magrady's age pissed off 'cause they figured it was those *mojados* who took away the decent jobs.

But Jeff Curray was still dead, and those two chuckleheads, Boo Boo the discount store psycho and the slicker Elmore Jinks were on the prowl. They were the rocks in his bed as the old song went. Something had gone down and signs indicated Floyd Chambers was all up in the shit—for there was the SubbaKhan magnetic swipe card.

Magrady had placed it on the kitchen table as he sipped his coffee, glancing at it occasionally as if he'd get a flash of insight. Too bad that unlike the classic reoccurring bit Johnny Carson did, Karnak, he couldn't slap the card to his forehead and get a clue.

He stretched and yawned and scratched his crotch. That's not something Dick Tracy or the Lone Wolf ever did in those

'40s B-reelers he still got a kick out of watching. Could be he was off his nut, but he'd proceed as if he were on point. Circling back to the Hornet's Hive later today was useless at this time even if the old fella, Sanford, did find an address for the sister. Of course the way things were going, he glumly concluded, it would probably turn out to be yet another far off location.

Given his luck, it would be out in San Bernardino or some damn other county that might as well be Pluto as far as his means to get there were concerned. Plus he wanted to be ready should he have to do the cha-cha with the two thugs again. He'd been considering retrieving his service sidearm. But that meant a reunion with his daughter and, well, that required more *cojones* than he could swing at the moment.

This left him with the SubbaKhan magnetic swipe card as his most immediate lead—and the most obtuse. It wasn't like he could go over to the SubbaKhan offices in their high-rise in Century City and test it out to see which door the thing opened. He knew from Bonilla there was serious security to contend with in the lobby.

In Long Beach, SubbaKhan owned Bixby Stadium where pro soccer games and, of all things, polo matches were played. Seems some wheel at SubbaKhan had a jones for the horsey sport and funded an amateur polo league. Magrady snickered imagining Bonilla and her comrades discussing a polo field for the at-risk youth of South Central as part of the community benefits agreement. Indeed, horses galloping and mallets a-swinging down Western Avenue. Though there was street polo played on bicycles so who knew? She'd also told him about a research effort the conglomerate had funded, but she wasn't sure where.

He showered and decided to go the library and find out more about SubbaKhan. It beat sitting around waiting for Redding's call. Indulging himself, he used some of Bonilla's fru-fru shampoo on his bristly short hair. Lathering the scented goo into his scalp, he felt the spot on the top of the back of his head. Was the hair getting thinner there? Alas, one more advancing age symptom to fret about.

Dried off and in his boxers, he laid across the bed staring at one of her posters, a silkscreened print of a solemn Nelson

Mandela. Yet political stirrings weren't energizing him as they should, and he got out of the bedroom before he sunk to sniffing through her underwear drawer. He shaved in the kitchen listening to KNX, the news station.

Done, Magrady stepped into clean jeans—he'd been able to wash his gear in her laundry room—and a buttoned-down shirt Bonilla had given him before she left this morning. She hadn't explained whose shirt it had belonged to previously. Magrady, a 2XLer, was pleased that it fit and wasn't snug. Now what did that say about her taste in men? Or big women?

He felt almost felt like a square on his way to his slave. Only it was after 9:30 a.m., and it was more like the leisurely pace those young punks on that show, *Entourage,* maintained. Each episode their days were consumed with chasing tail and scoring weed. He'd seen three or four of the half hours on DVD at the James Wood Center in the common area. In fact, he'd watched them with Floyd Chambers, among others. They'd been amused and incensed by those pampered dudes and their antics.

Magrady had riffed then, was the show telling them what the down and out should aspire to? Chambers had added that like Baby Doc's wife Michelle, the downtown visionaries would start hoisting caged TVs up on street lamps. They'd loop vids of mink coats four deep in walk-in closets and racks of trendy shoes to make Imelda Marcos and Condie Rice jealous. The message being that if you applied yourself, all this could be yours, too.

Now it's one thing to be a dictator. It's another to rub the peasants' noses in it, what with the Marcoses and Baby Doc being bounced from their respective homelands. But was Chambers inspired by these excesses? Magrady considered soberly.

He mused on this as he closed and locked the kitchen window in preparation of leaving his friend's homey digs. L.A. was where dreams were served along with your fresh-squeezed orange juice. There was desire and envy for the Hiltons and the Pitts. We built them up so they'd fall further when we kicked the stepladders out from under them—this the sport of kings and queens. No wonder nobody gave two shits about the homeless. What hopes and dreams could you project on those poor fucks? Maybe Chambers did get his the best way he could.

Magrady exited through the back door, descending to a garden patch behind the apartment building containing raspberries, tomatoes and mustard greens. These were tended by an octogenarian tenant who'd once been a bookie. Heading north on Catalina, the Vietnam vet got to a bus stop on Wilshire and took one of the red and white Rapid buses into downtown.

He sat next to a young man with his hair frizzed out at numerous uncombed angles. He was listening to his iPod while reading a Philip K. Dick novel, *The Three Stigmata of Palmer Eldritch*. The youngster wore a Free the Buses T-shirt, a fight back effort Magrady had belonged to several years ago.

Back then with LRS and a couple of other public interest law firms committing to the cause, the grouping had legally challenged the transportation agency, the MTA. This was over the argument for more monies allocated for increasing clean buses on inner city routes. Magrady had been down with that. Though he found some of the enviros, as they were called, way too anal about the green thing. These diehards pushing in meetings for the suit to be a tactic toward abolishing buses in favor of rail, and thus more rail meant less cars.

The theory had merit as Magrady could see a combination of the two. But certainly folks needed those buses to get to their jive jobs, and knowing too that the MTA was inclined to construct rail servicing the better-off suburbs. It came down to too many meetings and pre-meetings being consumed with who had the correct analysis, and not enough being in the face of the MTA. Magrady was among several who dropped out. At that time he'd maintained he was taking a principled stance. Or was he just a cut-and-runner full of rhetoric and rationalizations? Like dodging and ducking his responsibilities when his family had depended on him.

Off the bus, walking along Flower toward the main library, an unmarked LAPD Crown Victoria passed him, the movement registering in the corner of his eye. The car double parked to a medley of horns honking and idled where he stood.

"What's happening, home folks?" Fuckin' Stover. He was dressed in civvies.

"What, I'm not walking fast enough for you? Gonna give me a ticket for loitering? Too bad I don't have a milk crate with me you can confiscate." The cops often took the shopping carts or milk crates of items from the homeless on the pretense they were stolen items. Only they rarely returned them to the stores, and dumped truckloads of the goods east of the L.A. River.

"Man, you sure are Mister Grumpy this morning. Me, I feel great." He grinned sterlingly. "Heard some of your *mojado*-running buddies got vamped on last night."

"I'm underwhelmed by your empathy."

The police captain laughed.

"I don't have time for your bullshit, Stover." He started to walk away.

"See you in court," the cop said cheerily and drove off.

What a giant A-1 asshole. Magrady walked up the steps of the Richard J. Riordan Central Library. In '86, two consecutive arson fires by even bigger assholes resulted in some 350,000 books being burned up and 700,000 being damaged. He remembered they had to freeze dry the remaining books to preserve them. Under the then Tom Bradley administration, air rights were sold to a developer to build the Library Tower to help pay for the massive renovation.

The seventy-three-story skyscraper looming over the main library was now called the U.S. Bank Tower. In 2001, the city's Library Commission, its members appointed by Riordan, who succeeded Bradley, voted to rename the wonderfully redone complex for hizzoner. The commissioners cited his tireless efforts in the service of libraries. Bradley got a wing named after him.

Magrady nodded to a couple of dudes he knew from the streets playing the Chinese game Go at a table in an alcove after he entered the facility. He had fond memories of coming here with his folks when he was a kid to look for the science fiction novels his old man liked to read. In those days there were massive statues of Egyptian gods built into the stair structure on the mezzanine level leading to the fiction section. He always saw them as the guardians of the magic found between those cracked covers by his pop's favorites like H. G. Wells and Jack Williamson. There was also those Edgar Rice Burroughs' John Carter of Mars and A. E. van Vogt books his mom would check out and discuss with him as well.

On a few sheets of unfolded paper, Magrady had a copy of various references for SubbaKhan culled from Lexis-Nexis. Bonilla had given him this as Urban Advocacy was always doing opposition research. She'd taken her laptop with her to the news conference and had no other computer at home. Using the printout as a basis, he looked through Google and micro-fiche files and found a year-old interview in the *Downtown News* with the regional VP of the entity, Wakefield Nakano, a Japanese-American local surfer boy from Gardena who made way good. A collector of modern art, he was the one overseeing the Emerald Shoals project. In the interview Nakano mentioned the policy project they'd just funded was located on the USC campus.

Magrady rode public transportation over to the campus and strolled onto it. He didn't much look like a student and he knew 'SC's campus cops didn't take no shit. But it was daytime and they were used to community people being there for this or that meeting, so he figured as long as he didn't go crazy and dry hump the Tommy Trojan statue, everything should be copacetic.

After stopping and asking several students and a janitor, he found the door to the Central City Reclaiming Initiative on the third floor of the business school. The project was spelled out in neat fourteen-point raised metal letters on the otherwise plain locked door. There was no response to his knocking. Retracing his steps, he'd noted a recessed metal door along the hallway. It was unmarked but had one of those electronic locks on it—the kind where you had to swipe a coded card through for entry.

Like Ronald Coleman as Raffles, he looked both ways along the quiet hallway and tried the magnetic card he'd found among Floyd Chambers' stuff. The red light on the lock turned green. Magrady let the light return to the closed setting. Once more he visually searched along the hallway for anyone coming or to see if he'd missed a security camera. Neither was in evidence. Nor could he detect any approaching footsteps, but how long would that last? Come on, do it he admonished himself. Man up, can't be a pussy now.

"Shit," Magrady mumbled as he swiped the mag card again, and again the electronic lock cleared. Using his shirttail, he took hold of the latch and opened the side door into the research office. He'd half expected the space to be laid out swank, given it was underwritten by SubbaKhan. Rather, the area he stepped into was plain and functionally drab. It was a narrow passageway with its length taken up by doors leading into various suites. At the near end was a wall and at the other a short hook around to some sort of reception area where the front door was. There were no pictures or prints on the walls.

He crooked his neck around to look for security cameras high up in the offices' corners. There weren't any, but that didn't mean they couldn't be hidden. But fuck it, he told himself, he was already breaking and entering, so if he was going to go down for his crime, he might as well make it worth the effort.

There were no names or suite numbers on any doors, and none of them, except one, was locked. Each office seemed to be a duplicate of the other, each containing a faux-woodgrain-topped metal desk, system-linked phones, computers with flat-screen monitors and, interestingly, no file cabinets. He fooled with the keyboard of one of the computers in rest mode but getting onto it was password protected. So much for unlocking the secrets of the Empire.

In another office he found a small framed photo on a desk. The shot was of a pretty, dark-skinned black woman with curly hair leaning down with her arms draped around a smiling Floyd Chambers in his wheelchair. He assumed this was his sister. Magrady sat down. There were a couple of other photos on the desk, one of a smiling young man in a graduation shot and another of a baby. A grandchild? Magrady frowned at the photo with Chambers. It seemed to him it was fairly recent but he wasn't sure about the age of the woman in it. And certainly there were cases of teenagers becoming mothers and then finding themselves as grandmothers in their late forties, so that could be the reason for the baby's picture. But he didn't think Chambers' sister had any children.

He looked through the drawers. It occurred to him as he sifted through yellow sticky pads, paper clips and staple containers, that playing detective made you feel entitled to invade other people's shit. Because after all you were after the big secret, so you were entitled to do anything in pursuit of the truth. He smiled.

In the bottom left-hand drawer on a stack of copier paper there was a set of keys. He was tempted to steal them but then that would only make him go off and search for the locks they fit. He could see himself then unlocking some other room somewhere else and inside that room would be a combination written on a piece of paper. That like some intricate set of Chinese puzzle boxes, one thing was inside the other, leading him on and on but no closer to Chambers and answers—if such were to be had.

He checked the time and used the phone. What the hell, it was a local number, how likely would it be to raise a flag when whoever it was paid the phone bill?

"How'd the strategy meeting go?" he asked Janis Bonilla when she answered.

"Where are you? The number's not coming up."

"I have my secrets."

"Be that way." She filled him in, including a push the groups were making to have a meeting with the police chief. He was about law and order, but also about his media image. While it was the feds who'd conducted the raid, the LAPD cooperated, so the coalition would make the chief the target. The idea being to have him in turn put pressure on ICE to respond.

"Oh, one of your honeys called," she added.

"You mean Halle's forgiven me?"

"I wouldn't know, Big Pimpin'," she cracked. "It was that Angie. Said she has news for you." It seemed to him there was a leering quality to her voice.

"How'd she get your number?"

"I guess she's got her secrets too. And your backward self needs to get a cell phone. I am hardly your damn answering service." Nonetheless, she gave him the number Angie Baine had left. She didn't ask if he'd be camping out at her place later and he didn't bring it up. Things were getting comfortable awfully quick.

Before making that call, feeling that time was tight, Magrady tried each key on the locked door but none of them fit. Back at the desk he assumed was Sally Prescott's, he replaced the keys and noted a lump under the copier paper. He pulled the sheets aside and spotted an unmarked cassette tape. He picked it up, examining it. Probably just an old-fashioned mix tape, he figured. Still.

Magrady was slipping the tape into his shirt pocket and actually gasped. The front door was being unlocked. Good thing the lights had been on when he'd entered. No sense crawling under the desk as his sorry black ass would stick out anyway. The door to the office he was in was only open a sliver as he'd unconsciously pushed it closed when he'd re-entered. He went stone and waited, breathing shallowly. Too many movies about life in the big house, including those episodes of *Oz* with their numerous anal rapes and other forms of male-on-male degradation, flickered rapidly inside his head. His one shining hope was that at his age, what booty bandit would want him? The real f'd up sociopaths of course. The Nazi Custom Chopper Brotherhood of Geranium Enthusiasts would pass him around like an unscented box of Kleenex.

The footsteps from beyond the door went past his room, the person humming. He wasn't sure but thought they stopped at the last room, the locked one. This was confirmed as Magrady heard a key turning in the lock and the door opening. A beat or two more, then a radio came on, an oldies station. Magrady started breathing again and eased the drawer closed, leaving the keys.

As Percy Sledge prognosticated in that down home sweat-and-grits growl of his that "They gonna find us, they gonna find us," Magrady tiptoed the office chair, which fortunately was on rollers, away from the desk. He leaned back to rise and the goddamn thing creaked. Did the twang of the guitars cover the noise? Magrady couldn't remain in this half-crouch for long so he stood erect and came around the desk. The song concluding, he stepped out of the office. The door to the last office was wide open. The side door he'd come through was in that direction and he'd been seen trying to get out that way. The front was his only option.

Despite the natural inclination to bolt, he crept forward on the industrial carpet, doing his best to lift his feet straight up and put them straight down to eliminate undue drag or sound. He peeked into the room, his back flat against the wall, as if that made him hard to see. From the position of the desk in the room, this person sat in profile to the doorway, the desk at ninety degrees to the doorway. His head was down as he made a handwritten notation and then stood, closing a file folder.

Magrady was pretty sure that was Wakefield Nakano, SubbaKhan's regional VP in there. Nakano put the file away in a standing file cabinet and locked it back. He returned to his desk and Magrady knew he was pushing it to stay any longer. He scuttled away and got his hand on the front door's knob when he could hear Nakano moving around again too. For sure the exec was also leaving. Worse, there were voices in the hallway beyond the door. Scared, but having no choice, Magrady stepped out as quickly as he could. He stood before the door, his back to it, closing it quietly.

A male and female student were walking past, deep in their conversation about Romney's versus Giuliani's strengths and weaknesses and the mystery as to why neither of their candidacies took off. Magrady headed for the stairs. To his back he heard the main door to the office open and Nakano exit as well.

Be cool, he reminded himself, making sure to proceed at a normal pace. Nakano's footfalls were a hurried cadence behind him. If he was busted, wouldn't the VP yell "halt" or "freeze" like they did on TV? The exec had a couple of decades on Magrady, so could be he was just going to tackle him and make him piss and drool while jamming a stun gun to his nuts.

"Excuse me," Nakano said, as he moved past Magrady, bumping him slightly on the shoulder.

"No problem," the vet replied.

"Yes, of course," SubbaKhan's man said in a hushed voice. "I'm very interested in the Portinari." Magrady watched Nakano descend, one of those Bluetooth gadgets stuck in his ear.

He got to the bottom of the stairwell and dashed through the glass door of the business school, saying into the air, "That's not going to be a problem. I'll see to that." With that Nakano was gone.

Magrady also reached the ground floor berating himself for not having a car to tail the VP. What would Magnum or Mannix have to say about that? He also realized he hadn't called Angie. But as this was a college campus, finding a pay phone wasn't as hard as on the streets. He clinked his coins in and called the number Baine had given Bonilla.

"Earl," a man's voice said.

He was one of the bartenders at the King Eddy, a semi-dive, semi-hip bar in the King Edward Hotel on East 5th Street. Magrady knew all the watering holes in and orbiting Skid Row, and a fair amount between there and South Central. He'd certainly done his best to turn his kidneys into pâté in several of them. Years ago, before he too joined the "Am I a Murderer?" public guess-o-rama, Robert Blake filmed part of his TV cop show *Baretta* there as the supposed East Coast place where he lived. Magrady was a background extra—supernumerary bum was how it was described in the script—in a few episodes. A director told him he was a natural.

Magrady identified himself and asked about Angie.

"She said if you called, Sergeant Fury, to meet her at Hogarth's at 6:30 tonight."

"Why?"

"Like I give a shit. Get a goddamn cell phone like everyone else." The diplomatic Earl hung up.

Hogarth's wasn't a bar. It was a coffee house located near the Japanese American Cultural and Community Center off of 1st Street and Alameda. Where the encroachers, the downtown small dog-walkin', inner peace-seekin', loft-living crowd hung, Magrady reflected wryly. Why the hell would she be having him there and at that time?

Having several hours to fill, Magrady sought out a cassette recorder. He walked over to the Bethune Branch Library on Vermont. They did have one such model used for older versions of books-on-tape. Only it was on the fritz, though the librarian assured him that there was a laid off gentleman—a tinkerer as she put it—would be coming in to fix it this week-end. From there he walked over to Exposition Park and decided to take in an exhibit about '30s-era jazz clubs at the California African American Museum. This included a recreated section of the Club Alabam.

Standing in the tableau, a mellow croon by Billy Eckstine filled the space. When he was a kid, he had an uncle, husband of his mom's sister, who'd lived out here and visited the family in Chicago in the summer. Uncle Calvin would sit around drinking Hamms and Pabst beer, playing dominoes with his father and his friends, telling stories about Central Avenue, the Stem, from back in the day. Later, eating his fries at a McDonald's inside the Science Center, he watched a group of kids ohhing and ahhing on some kind of school outing. Time was tight indeed.

Because of traffic and the work around the Emerald Shoals project, he got back downtown on the bus to the coffee house late. There they were showing a '60s four-waller, *The Brain Invaders*. Angie Baine was second-billed with John Agar as some sort of scientist to his military man. She of course also falls in love with him, but has to electrocute him atop Mount Wilson after he's turned into a brain eater. All part of some Russki she-nanigans it seemed. The audience dug it.

Afterward, with Angie seated up front and looking pretty together, she answered questions and signed copies of a book about B-movie actresses that included a write-up about her and some cheesecake shots. Magrady looked through the coffee table book and stopped appreciatively on a shot of a nude Baine, hair up in a beehive, in an old-fashioned bathtub filled with liquefied chocolate. Seductively she munched on a giant strawberry with several of the fruit sprinkled about in the chocolate.

"Bet you figured I'd be wasted, huh?" she told him as he came up to congratulate her as the crowd filtered away.

"Well," he began.

"You've inspired me, Magrady. I wasn't drinking at the King Eddy. But I was on my way to get my hair done, and knew Earl would at least let me make a call." She squeezed his hand. "Glad you came."

"Yeah, this was great, Angie."

"You can be sweet when you want to be." She kissed him on the neck.

An octogenarian who'd been hanging back clomped over using his walker. He had on a turtleneck, a wig worse than what Phil Spector had dared to wear in court, and a large medallion on a heavy gold plated chain around his neck. Baine smiled weakly at him and the old fella socked Magrady in the gut. It wasn't much of a blow.

"This is him, isn't it? This is the swingin' dick bastard you're schtupping these days?"

Angie Baine giggled and Magrady took a step back. The clown with the bad rug might not be a candidate for an AARP-sanctioned boxing match, but he wasn't inclined to take another punch, no matter how anemic, to his stomach.

"Be cool, Jeremy," she said to the senior citizen. "You don't want to stroke out."

"Who is this chump?" Magrady asked, eyebrow raised.

"He adds yet another insult to his affronts." His arms shook his walker. "Who am I," he mocked.

"Jeremy was the director-producer of *Brain Invaders* among other such efforts," Baine illuminated, touching the old-ster's shoulder. This instantly put a calming effect on him, and he relaxed.

"Then how come you weren't at the screening, Coppola?"

"I was getting my pole waxed, Cool Breeze," he groused at Magrady.

"Look here, dad," Magrady started, thumping Jeremy's medallion with the back of two fingers. It depicted in bas-relief a nude couple doing it 69-style. Real classy. "Shouldn't you be more concerned with how many times a day you need to take your blood pressure pills?" He couldn't help it. Ever since he was a teenager, when a guy tried to make time with a girl of his, he'd have to show he wasn't a punk. Bad old habits died awfully hard.

Baine twinkled a smile at him. "Stop."

Jeremy whatever the hell his last name was said, "Baby, let's let the past stay where it belongs. You know I'll do right by you. Fact, I've got a movie in mind that I want you for as the lead."

"Get real, Jer, those days are long gone," Baine advised.

He smiled with freshly scrubbed dentures. "I'm serious, Angie. Some youngsters over at 'SC film school had me over there for a double bill at the Norris Theater on campus, and we got to talking after the Q & A." He shuffled his body closer so as to insert himself between Baine and Magrady.

"You know those rich little shits over there. A couple of these kids got parents in the Industry. One of them has called me since and wants to talk about me doing some direct-to-video pictures."

It was Baine's turn to arch a brow. "With an old broad as the star?" She laughed heartily. "I don't do granny porn, Jeremy." She winked at Magrady. "At least not for the public."

The crusty director made a sound in his throat. "I'm not that hard up to get back behind the camera. This is legit. Hell, I'll give Magic Mandingo here a role if that's what it'll take."

"I got your sister's Magic Mandingo right here, Jer."

The object of his derision turned slightly, wearing a lop-sided smile. "Yes, I'm sure you do."

"Boys," Baine said to forestall another go-round. She put her hand in the crook of Magrady's arm. "It was good seeing you again, Jeremy."

The ancient filmmaker repositioned himself on his walker as the couple started to leave. "Let me repeat that I'm not kidding about this, Ange. I'm not so deluded to believe this is some sort of comeback, but wouldn't it be nice to go out on a high note?"

She squeezed Magrady's upper arm. "The moonlight stopped shining on us a long time ago, Jeremy."

He pointed a gnarled finger upward. "There might be just one more in the firmament for us."

Baine offered Magrady a resigned look and wrote down a contact number on the back of a discarded parking lot ticket and handed it to Jeremy. His teeth clacked as he smiled broadly. The two left, the night cooler than expected. She snuggled closer.

"You gonna spend the night?"

"If you like," he said warmly.

She kissed him. "I do." They walked deeper into the Nickel like kids out on Lover's Lane. They passed a skeleton-thin man in a derby defecating in an alleyway and a woman with very few teeth padded in clothes of mismatched styles pushing a shopping cart. Leaning in the cart was a three-foot-tall plaster statue of a brightly painted Ann-Margaret in go-go boots and miniskirt circa the 1970s.

Magrady put an arm around Baine's shoulders just as an LAPD cruiser drifted near. It was one of the newer Chevy Commodore models. The uniforms put the alley light on them to make sure the burly black man wasn't manhandling the nice white lady. Or was Stover keeping that close of a watch on him? Magrady worried. Was that being paranoid or precautious?

"You okay, ma'am?" one of the cops asked, putting the wolf's gleam on Magrady.

"I'm fine," Baine smiled, waving them off. They kept the light on the couple for several more beats, then drove off. Further up the patrol car illuminated two Grape Street Crips and the cops stopped and detained the gangbangers.

As they walked along, Bain said, "Say, I also called you because Floyd got in touch."

"He wants that pass card back, doesn't he?"

"You're a regular Nick Carter."

"Ain't I? You tell him I had it?"

"Of course not. I'm your Velda, right?"

They both chuckled. "He's coming by?"

"Said for me to meet him 'round one tomorrow at that farmer's market they have up at the VA in Westwood."

Magrady regarded her.

Her shoulders lifted and fell. "Don't ask me. Maybe he wanted to avoid Asher." She referred to the one-armed desk clerk at her SRO. "They don't get along."

"More likely he's staying out that way."

"See, you are a clever dick."

"I hope you mean that in a good way. And you know for a woman your age you sure talk . . . suggestively."

"It doesn't seem to bother you."

"This is so."

To be polite he called Janis Bonilla from a phone at the Midnight Mission. A case worker Magrady had done a favor for let him do so.

After some chit-chat, Bonilla cracked, "You got all the dames worried about you, huh?"

"Good night, Janis."

"Good night, Gracie."

Magrady was relieved that Asher wasn't on the desk at the Chesapeake, though he'd encountered him there during nighttimes in the past. Getting into a hassle now when he was hankering to direct his energies elsewhere would just be a drag. Concentration was everything.

Sure the rules were no guests after 8 p.m. but plenty of clerks, unlike the anal Asher, let you violate that rule—particularly if you offered money or booze or a hit of something stronger as thanks. In this case, El Cid, Sid Ramos, was on duty. He was a mellow fellow veteran as far as Magrady was concerned.

"Em," he said in that rasp of his, knocking a fist with his friend. He'd been over there before Magrady, a homeboy from El Sereno who wound up being a Lurp, an LRRP, a long range reconnaissance patrol maniac. These were men who operated in small teams, going deep in country to scout air strike targets and do recon. It took a certain type who liked being alone with their doubts and fears for days on end yet remain coiled. El Cid had engaged in various activities when he got back to the world, including a jolt in the pen.

Magrady retorted, "It bees like that." He grinned at El Cid as the two moved past. The desk man returned to reading his book, *The Last Cavalier*, by Alexandre Dumas. As Magrady understood it back in his time, while Dumas was in bad shape and his work out of favor with the critics, but not the masses, he couldn't help but do his thing and churned out a daily serial in a newspaper. Nowadays some pipe-smoking academic had come along and put the chapters together and edited them as the last novel by the cat who created the Three Musketeers. Magrady realized these knot-head, pants-saggin' kids only knew the Musketeers as the name of a candy bar, let alone Dumas was part black.

Damn youngsters didn't know squat these days, Magrady lamented as Baine slowly stroked him as they kissed. Thereafter they went at it like caged minks.

IV

BEFORE LIGHT THE NEXT MORNING, and after another invigorating thrash with the able Ms. Baine, Magrady dreamed of Vietnam. But this wasn't a sweaty rehash of a firefight or reliving yet again the horror of watching some greenie writhing in the mud holding his guts in while being held down by his comrades as the medic tried to super glue the wounds closed.

This was an incident on base where a Japanese-American sergeant was walking from the outdoor showers with a towel wrapped around his waist. Two freshly rotated in replacements, one black, one white, saw him and freaked out. "VC! VC!" they started hollering, with the excited black GI bringing up his M-60 to spray the sergeant.

"Hey, you goddamn idiot," the sergeant swore, "I went to Dorsey High School in Los Angeles."

"He's trying to trick us," the white one told his buddy.

Magrady had spotted this and with some others had already run over and stopped the altercation before blood flowed.

The sergeant shook his head afterward. "JAFS," he said. To Magrady's puzzled look he illuminated, "Just Another Fucked-up Situation."

They both chuckled as the man went off to get dressed in his uniform. What ever happened to those two chuckleheads, Magrady couldn't say. But that JA sergeant, whose name was Yoshida, became a public defender. This he knew as during one of his lost periods, by the randomness of the cosmic wheel, Yoshida had been assigned by his office to represent Magrady after he'd been arrested for trespassing—while tore up on coke and booze.

"You don't remember," the attorney had said after interviewing Magrady in jail about his case.

"I do," he admitted, ashamed. "I just hoped you didn't remember me."

The other man nodded his head. "It's JAFS, Magrady. You're not the first one of us I've helped whose had some bad luck after coming back to the world. We'll get past this and take it from there."

Sure enough he got a return engagement back in rehab coupled with a community service sentence reduction. Yoshida had him placed with Community Now, a grassroots organization his wife sat on the board of in those days. Eventually, due partly to strategic planning and partly to infighting, Community Now would become Urban Advocacy

Daybreak, he in his boxers and Baine in a slip, the two lay together in bed listening to a Bartók CD. Her head on his torso, Baine asked him, "You think about your kids?"

He massaged her butt. Considering her seven-plus decades, it was quite a lovely sensation. But at his age, Magrady could squeeze fresh bread and get a thrill. "Yeah, a lot recently." It probably would break the mood to tell her partly because he had his gun at his oldest's house out in Diamond Bar.

"You?" She had a grown son she hadn't seen for some time. A lying, cheatin'-ass doper he recalled from bitter experience.

"Chad got word to me. Says he's clean and lean."

"Who says?"

"His chick who came by."

"That you lent a twenty to, I bet."

She kissed his chest. "Thirty, darling."

"Sheeeet."

"He was at work. She showed me a picture on her cell phone. He's a security guard at the Emerald Shoals site."

"Then he should be able to come by and see you."

"He will."

Magrady didn't want to cause static. We all needed something to hang onto.

As several strings and drums went wild on the record then settled into a moody dissonance, Baine let her hand go low on his body and damned if he wasn't able to soldier up. This was also why he didn't argue with her about her son. He figured she might be feeling frisky and why mess with that? Cialis? Viagra? Heh. He was Kong, son of Kong, baby.

When they were done he promised to call Baine this coming weekend, if only to prevent her taking up with that bastard Jeremy again he half-joked. Magrady got all stealthy coming down the hall and could see, as he feared, the one-armed Asher on the desk. He was doing a card trick with his pincer to keep himself amused. He flipped the king of hearts over in his metal grip then back and suddenly the face card was now a ten of clubs. Magrady was impressed but certainly wasn't going to clap.

At one point staying at the Chesapeake was a former stage magician who went by the name Greystone. He occasionally did gigs at the Magic Castle in Hollywood when his arthritis permitted. Being a magician who specialized in close work, like making coins fall through solid tables, required nimble fingers, yet he'd taught Asher a few tricks before he died of emphysema.

Going back the way he came, he passed Baine's room. From inside he could hear her pleasant voice hum and sing "Red River Valley." He got to the inside stairwell door and creaked it open. Asher would hear it but probably wouldn't pursue him in the stairwell, as this meant disturbing his practice session. Magrady came out on the side of the building in a narrow passageway crowed with trash and smelling ripe. He bought some tepid coffee from the Shell gas station quick mart and didn't give in to the lust to have a muffin. He walked over to the Urban Advocacy offices but Bonilla was in the field and the intern that had helped him, Fjeldstrom, wasn't around either. He was able to check for his mail and was surprised to find a letter for him.

"She must have strong ju-ju," he mumbled, meaning Angie Baine talking about her family had conjured up his as well. Magrady went back to the waiting area in front and sat heavily in one of the plastic chairs. Snakes writhing in his throat, he stared at the envelope. The letter was from his ex-wife, Claudelia. She'd long ago remarried and was now living in Tulsa, being an Oklahoma girl originally. He tapped it against his fingertips. He just knew this couldn't be good news.

He debated reading the message now or later. A woman who'd been there before him was now talking to one of the organizers about her unfair eviction. Magrady folded the letter and tucked it in his back pocket. One goddamn problem at a time, he reasoned. He went to the bus stop on Wilshire and after two other buses came and went, got the Line 10 of the blue bus, Big Blue it was nicknamed, the one he needed to take him far enough. This one took a freeway route and its riders tended to be dressed in suits and expensive shoes—lawyers doing their part at being eco friendly.

The Westwood Farmers Market was a once-a-week fresh food affair held in the fourteen-acre garden on the expansive Veterans Affairs facility off of Wilshire near the 405 Freeway. The garden also included rows of rose bushes, and gave recuperating vets an opportunity to do some head healing through the symbolic and practical act of growing fruits and vegetables. Magrady wasn't much on sod busting, but he appreciated what this program did for the vets.

He nodded at a twenty-some-year-old man in cargo shorts with one of those space age curved metal legs attached below his real knee. He watched the Iraqi vet offload some red potatoes from a van and continued walking about, searching for Floyd Chambers. He bought some strawberries from a vendor because weren't they a natural way to keep your pencil sharp? Seemed his dad used to say that. Stacked under the table's stall were several crates etched Shishido Farm in the soft wood.

Munching on his snack, he rounded another stall where a heavyset woman was using a screwdriver to undo the plastic straps sealing a cardboard box. He also spotted Chambers. He had on a floppy hat and was wheeling about, having just talked with a young woman holding a clipboard. Magrady was about to call to him but something clicked like those times in the war threading through jungle overgrowth. Damn if his Spidey Sense hadn't kicked in. Must be the way Floyd was looking around trying to seem casual but not. He followed his brief head turns to Boo Boo, he of the sunset eyes. His Yogi fortunately didn't seem to be about.

The thug was hefting a couple of husks of corn but he too was on alert. What had they intended to do to Angie, Magrady roiled moodily. Channeling his anger, he moved toward Boo Boo, having picked up the screwdriver from the vendor's table.

Magrady was behind and to the right of the Boo before he noticed him. He'd been distracted trying to mack on a smooth-skinned honey who had the good sense to not give him those digits. "How you doin', fuckhead?" he said while simultaneously jabbing the screwdriver into the hoodlum's lower side. He wasn't looking to puncture a kidney, just get a response.

"Motherfuck," Boo Boo hollered, squinting then going wide-eyed at the sight of the evilly grinning vet. "That's your ass, old man."

He lunged for Magrady, who immediately dropped to the ground and went into a fetal position. He yelled, "Oh my God, he attacked me. Help! Help!" His plastic bag of strawberries smashed into gooey red pulp beneath him.

Boo Boo was dependable. "Shut the fuck up," he bellowed, aiming the points of his too-clean Jordans towards Magrady's stomach. Anticipating such, the other man had X'd his forearms in front of his body. Three of the VA's security guards who were weaving about in the farmer's market ran over.

"He just went crazy," Magrady avowed, "I'm a veteran and he hates vets, he said."

"Hey wait," Boo Boo started as one of the guards, who'd

recently taken the Sheriff's exam and was anxious to learn the results, tackled him.

Magrady scooted out to the way. He had to give Boo Boo his props. At first as the guards swarmed him, he went on instinct and fought back. But even in what passed for a mind atop the hoodlum's thick neck understood the hole he'd been placed in, and further action on his part was only sucking him down deeper. He became compliant.

Problem was the guards were amped and as Double B declared, "I give," the would-be deputy Tasered him in the side of his neck. His legs and arms convulsed and he swore a string of profanities, with some particular illustrative language aimed at Magrady and his kin. They got him to his feet, his legs the consistency of overcooked pasta.

"Mister, you okay?" one of the earnest young protectors asked. He was taller than Magrady with a country-boy Norman Rockwell look about him.

"Yes, I think so." Magrady iced the cake. "For some reason he singled me out. I think he'd seen me here before, he knew I was a Vietnam vet." That would set him in solid with these guys. "Walking around mumbling about how the marines wouldn't take him 'cause of some sort of criminal charge."

"You lying shitfaced bitch-ass punk," Boo Boo screamed. "I'll fix you for this."

"Keep quiet," the deputy hopeful said as he used metal cuffs on the bargain-store gangster. They bent him over a table with boxes of mushrooms on it and patted him down.

"Look, we're going to take him in and see if he has any priors," the embodiment of all-Americanism said. "We saw him attacking you."

"So did I," a woman in pedal pushers holding a plastic sack of tomatoes said. "He simply went Rambo on this poor man." She looked about, embarrassed. "Sorry, I didn't say that right."

The guard continued, "Look, you might have to swear out a complaint for the police, so we'll need to get in touch with you."

"Not a problem." Magrady gave him the address and phone for the Urban Advocacy offices. He shook the earnest guard's hand and went in search of Floyd Chambers. At the start of the trouble, he'd wheeled away. Magrady figured they'd come in Boo Boo's car, and that he'd be able to track him on foot in the vicinity. He hoped too that Boo Boo did have unanswered charges or bench warrants for traffic tickets so the cops would keep him locked up at least for a few days. Once he got out . . . well . . . that was once he got out. Too bad the roughneck hadn't brought his heater with him. Guess he wasn't that stupid, Magrady concluded.

Huffing it out to Wilshire Boulevard, Magrady spotted Chambers on the other side of the street heading east, away from the VA and the soldier's graveyard where several of Magrady's comrades were buried. This part of the thoroughfare was wide and given the entrance and exits of the 405 freeway, the traffic was steady with assorted vehicles and buses. "How the hell did he get over there so quick?" Magrady mumbled.

Neither a stoplight nor a crosswalk were immediately available. But he couldn't let him slip away now so he timed it and darted into the street. Drivers braked and swerved and gave him the finger or cursed him.

He went around the rear of an accordion bus and made it to the other side, a motorcyclist blaring, "Idiot grandpa. Get back to your rest home."

Chambers' arms were churning and he wheeled swiftly under the overpass. Magrady jogged after him, aware he was breathing harder than he'd like to be. He slowed his pace but kept on as Chambers worked his wheels with a practiced flourish. On the south side of Wilshire east of the overpass was the Federal Building where such offices including passport and the FBI were located. There was a contingent of protestors in front, which was not unusual, except this was a weekday in the mid-afternoon. Who the hell would be out now?

Magrady had to assume it was anti-war stalwarts. But as he dashed through the smattering of people he noted a sign with a cut out of a lazing polar bear on it with the words "Save Them" printed on it. Another read, "Stop Global Warming. More Ice for the Bears." Swell sentiment, he reflected as he watched Chambers roll to the other side of the true believers. Did they expect the Bureau to drop their current caseload and build rafts for the polar bears?

He felt guilty for being a cynical asshole, but there would have to be another time to save the glaciers. Magrady took some deep breaths and got his arms and legs pumping . . . The one thing Magrady could do to close the space was cut across the huge lawn of the Federal Building. Chambers had to stick to the sidewalk for better traction.

"Come on, Floyd," he yelled, running across the grass, "hold up. What's the deal, man?" He prayed that there weren't twenty-four-hour snipers on duty on the roof just waiting for some nut to sound vaguely threatening so they could relieve their boredom by misting his brains.

The disabled man glanced at him then kept on trucking toward Ohio Street. Magrady could feel his burst of energy dissipating and laughed inwardly at those who said age was just a number. Shit. Age was your body letting you down and sweat pouring out of you like a bucket with a hole in it. Fuck if he wasn't going to get away from him, a chump in a wheelchair. Okay, he admitted, that wasn't being touchy-feely either. But getting pissed gave him focus and renewed energy. Magrady, never one for the treadmill, put all he had left in a last effort to catch his fleeing friend.

"Watch it, lady," Chambers hollered as he went off the curb and tried to cross in the middle of the street. A young woman illegally talking on her handheld cell phone, Mariah Carey rockin' on her car's sound speakers, had turned onto Ohio from the far corner and roared toward Wilshire in her late model Mustang. She was too wrapped up in her conversation to see Chambers until she was on him.

She slammed to a halt. Floyd's gloved hands locked on his wheels and he fishtailed his wheelchair into the side of the driver's door. Chambers fell over. The young woman, a strawberry blonde with heavy mascara scolded, "Dude, look what you did to my door." She was staring down at Chambers, on his side, in the street next to his downed wheelchair.

"What he did to you?" Magrady said, running up, out of breath. "You just ran over a disabled man, miss. We need the police to test you for marijuana or ecstasy or something." Gasping, he continued, "I saw everything. You never once slowed down, and you were illegally talking on your cell phone. No hands-free set."

The pretty woman screwed up her face at him then looked past to the bear lovers who'd also come over. "Wait, what are you saying?"

"You know damn well what I'm saying," Magrady helped Chambers, also breathing hard, sit up and righted his chair. "You're going to jail. You're a menace."

"Maybe I should call my lawyer."

"Yeah, I do think you should call mommy and daddy's lawyer. And I'll get some witnesses' statements while you're at it." He got Chambers into his wheelchair. "How are you, sir? Can you understand the words coming out of my mouth?" He over-enunciated, stealing the line from that comedy movie with Chris Tucker and Jackie Chan.

He muttered to Magrady, "Crazy motherfucker." He rasped out loud, "I think I'll be okay." It didn't escape him that Magrady had a grip on the handle of his chair.

"Well, your medical bills should be added to the lawsuit," he said louder than necessary. "You'll need to get checked out thoroughly."

The driver had put a sandal-clad foot on the ground preparing to step out of her car but froze at that statement. "He's all right," she insisted, looking from Chambers to her dented door.

"Really?" Magrady challenged. "We better let a doctor determine that."

She sat in the car again, closing the door. It creaked. Several drivers slowed to rubberneck then went around them in the street. "There's no need for that."

"Aren't you going to get your mouthpiece on the phone? I want to talk to him," Magrady said authoritatively. He hedged this behavior would have her backing down.

"He's okay, right?" the young woman asked.

"I'm not saying that," Magrady answered.

"I'm asking him," she retorted irritably.

"I can make it," Chambers said.

She started the Mustang. "So let's just call it even." Putting it into gear, the vehicle slowly crept forward as the onlookers watched her go.

"I've got her license number," one of the good citizens shouted. She looked to be the same age as the driver, but tanned, wearing a short T that exposed her taut belly and the jewel stud in her navel. She stepped forward and handed Magrady the information on the back of a crumpled receipt. He thanked her and she displayed very even teeth. She was cute. Magrady got back on task.

Mustang Sally took all this in but continued going. She got to the corner and then turned east into the afternoon flow.

"I'll make sure he gets home okay." Magrady said and half-waved to the concerned.

"I can take him to a doctor," the nice tanned lady said. "He might have internal injuries or who knows what."

Magrady squeezed Chambers' shoulder blade, grinning.

"Thank you, but I'm fine. It's okay." Chambers got the message. Doubtless too he didn't want to be hung up at some emergency room or clinic for several hours. He and his lowlife buddies were hunting in the tall grass, Magrady reasoned, and he intended to find out what kind of game they were after.

"Now I'm going to wheel your ass over here," Magrady was close to his friend's ear, pushing him at a normal speed across the side street, away from the bear patrol.

Chambers licked his lower lip. "How come you're all up in this, Magrady?"

"Why'd you try to vamp on Angie?'

"It's not like that, man. She's been straight with me. I just wanted—" but he didn't finish.

They got to the curb and Magrady turned the chair around and cocked it back to pull the wheelchair up and onto the grass strip of the sidewalk. Behind him was a row of grey and white apartment buildings.

"Then why are you and Boo Boo making like Starsky and Hutch?"

"I had no choice."

The two moved further into the residential section. "You need to let me know what the hell's going on, Floyd." They went along some. "This has something to do with your sister, doesn't it?"

Chambers looked off to one side. "You talked to her?"

"No. But I know she works for that division of SubbaKhan."

"What else do you know?"

"That my sorry self has a possible murder beef hanging over me."

"They can't make it stick. You know that."

Magrady said, "I know that Stover will be giving it the ol' college try." He stopped pushing him and coming around in front, clamped his hands on both of Chambers' shoulders, leaning into him. "What the hell are you up to, Floyd? You know me, I don't give a fuck what kind of scam you're setting up or trying to run." He let go of him. "But you ain't gonna make me your goat. You got me involved in this shit when you used me to go up against Savoirfaire then all of a sudden he winds up dead."

"You sayin' I did that?"

"I'm saying that's a mighty funny coincidence."

Chambers worked his wheels back and forth, his face downcast. "It's not like I don't think you're down, Magrady. But this, this could be big."

"Big how?"

He smiled, his eyes lit up like he was faded on weed. "The rainbow, baby."

Magrady was tired of this bullshit. "I've got your magnet card and the cassette tape, Floyd."

That deflated his balloon. "I need that tape, Em. I guess you haven't played it yet, huh?"

"What if I burn it?"

Chambers held up a hand. "We can work something out."

"What's the play, Floyd?"

For a moment it seemed he might try to bolt again. Instead, he took in a deep breath. The two had stopped partially up the incline of a rising street, the kind where the garages were set below the house and cut into the hillside. He motioned with his hands. "It's, you know, it's what they dug up."

"Like lost treasure?" Magrady almost laughed.

His friend nodded quickly. "Yeah."

Now he did laugh. "Come on, Floyd. You're after Blackbeard's treasure chest?"

"The item was dug up at the Emerald Shoals. Only they didn't know what they had. Not exactly."

A tickle feathered Magrady's spine. "But your sister found out what this was and she told you?"

Chambers shook his head. "It's wild, Magrady, wild as sin."

"The hell, Floyd? What are you going on about?"

Chambers adopted a cagey look. "I've already said too much."

"Uh-huh. So what's this have to do with Savoirfaire getting iced?"

The disabled man hunched his shoulders. "I figured that was Boo Boo's and Elmore's doing. But now I don't know for sure." He frowned.

The two were moving along the residential street, fine particles of ash dusted the parked cars and trees. Magrady sniffed the air but detected no burnt smell and wondered what had produced the residue. Was there a fire somewhere or was this some kind of sign portending coming events? The image of the young man reading the Philip K. Dick novel on the bus floated through his head. This caused him to softly panic, imagining he was really some sort of character wrought from Dick's meth-addled mind. That he merely dreamed he was real while trapped in a time loop forever doomed to repeat this futile search over and over again, while not gaining any insight whatsoever in any of his incarnations.

Magrady asked, "Then why'd you go all subterranean?"

Chambers steadily pumped the wheels of his chair, his hands fluid and seamless in their repetitive motion. "I figured those two were moving in on his territory and would be taking over Savoirfaire's book." He glanced up. "I know you see yourself as six ways to bad, Em, but those two are money crazy."

The explanation sounded plausible but Magrady knew his friend was holding back. Savoirfaire had attacked him with a hook knife, and if that wasn't a demonstration he was as homicide happy as the Wonder Twins, then what did? But he played along by saying, "And what made it different when our boy Boo found you? And by the way, where have you been keeping yourself?"

They'd come to a corner and reflexively, both turned north toward Wilshire again. "I got associates all over town, man," Chambers joked. "Maybe I was laying up with the even finer cousin of Eva Mendes 'cause she likes to get her freak on with a dead leg'd man." He leaned back and did a 360-degree donut, laughing.

Dryly Magrady said, "Anything you say, Floyd."

"Friend of a friend, okay?"

"How'd butthead find you?"

Chambers grinned. "I guess I need to enlarge my circle."

Magrady grabbed the wheelchair's handles, causing Chambers' gloved hands to skid on his wheels' high impact rubber. "Answers, Floyd. Stop fucking around. Or I dump you out here and take this thing with me." He shook the wheelchair, gritting his teeth. They were in the middle of the block leading back to the main thoroughfare.

Chambers stared at his angry friend, deciding if the other man was bullshitting or not. He took in an audible breath. "I was staying at a few places where I could beg a night, even had to sleep out at the beach a couple of nights." He did a quick head jerk to the west.

"Not only is it nasty when you're stuck in a chair, but you don't know what fool that's off his meds is sneaking around out there up to devilment. Wound up in a kind of shelter near there, Santa Monica I mean. It's actually just some rooms above that church run by that lefty pastor that has those meetings out there. Met him through Janis."

"I know who you mean," Magrady said, "Reverend Conn."

"That's where that sadistic mufu Boo found me. Seems him and his crime partner put the promise of product as reward on the street, and you know them crackheads would sell their mama's left titty for some rock." The two reached Wilshire. "One of them sported me and dimed me out. Next thing I knew homeboy showed up demanding the money I owed Savoirfaire." He gestured feebly with his hands. "I tried to tell him you cleared that up but he wasn't having it."

"So you were gonna have him knock Angie in the head, man?"

Chambers evidenced a pained expression. "I ain't that low, Magrady."

"Then what was the deal?"

"I was buying time. He was gonna hang back like you saw and I'd get the mag card from her."

"What did Boo Boo think you were going to take him to? This mysterious windfall you keep hinting at?"

Chambers rolled on thoughtfully then, "I had to do something, man, you know how he gets. I told him there was cash that I could get by using the card." Continuing along he added, "But I made sure not to say shit to him about the cassette tape and what it, well," he paused, not wishing to say more, "what it was."

"Even homeboy can't be so gone on his chronic that he believed that a big company like SubbaKhan kept money lying around." Magrady decided to keep Chambers focused on the procedural stuff rather than press him on what this grail of his was. He hoped to angle back to the mysterious prize at some point once he got his friend talking.

"He didn't know what kind of door the card opened. I convinced him my sister worked at a finance operation of SubbaKhan. So, you know, he just assumed there'd be money in a strong box or something."

They'd halted on Wilshire, near the busy intersection of Westwood Boulevard. A group of young women walked by, one in tight sweatpants with "Juicy" in pink Gothic letters arched over her bouncy butt. Two of them had ear buds in leading to their iPods they thumbed selections on, and simultaneously maintained a conversation with the others. He found it hard to believe that Boo and Elmore had chased Chambers all over town just to shake him down for what? A few hundred dollars at the most? Sure those two were swap meet special gangstas, but were they that hard up?

Magrady asked, "What did you mean that you don't think they killed Savoirfaire?"

Chambers squinted up at him. "Your good buddy Boo was talkin' too much like he does and was saying to Elmore he figured you for Savoirfaire's killer. Yeah, they took advantage of a good situation from their viewpoint, but it sounded like they were as surprised as anyone else when he got done in."

Magrady considered this and said, "We gotta come to an understanding, Floyd."

The paraplegic rolled his chair a few feet forward then back, his version of pacing. "You give me the tape back and I tell you about what was dug up."

"That's about right."

"I'll have to get back to you on that, Em."

"I guess that means you'll talk this over with your sister."

Chambers nodded.

Magrady had already calculated that it didn't seem like it had been cash or jewels from some long ago robbery that had been recovered, as even a child would know such was valuable and would not have turned the swag over to anyone else. He assumed it was a construction worker on the Emerald Shoals project who initially unearthed this thing. Too, the dingus may not have been in the brother's and sister's possession from the way Chambers was acting. Or it had been but wasn't now. The tape was possibly some clue to getting it back? And from whom? This detective business could make a man weary, he sighed inwardly.

"I don't hear from you in two days, Floyd, then maybe I have to make other arrangements."

Chambers' muscular upper body stiffened. "Jesus, Magrady, why you got to be such a stiff prick about this?"

He pointed at him. "Because you're playing me and the Sunshine Boys for chumps, Floyd. Now them that's fine, but we've been through some shit. I don't deserve this." He was surprised at the emotion in his words.

Chambers held up a hand. "Look, man. Just let me talk to sis and we'll get straight on this. Just don't mess up that tape."

"You better get back to me."

"Where can I catch you?"

Magrady told him to leave a message at the Urban Advocacy offices. Chambers rolled west and Magrady walked east. He found a pristine pay phone—figures on this side of town he reflected—and made a call to Gordon Walters, the mouthpiece assigned to his case at Legal Resources and Services of Greater Los Angeles.

"Yo, Gordy," he said after amenities, "you know any

particulars about how Savoirfaire was killed, aside from him getting his head beat in?"

"Not that I can recollect, but let me go through my notes. The deputy D.A. on this case is not fast-tracking this, which can be good. But that also might mean they're looking to gather enough to make the charge stick against you. Anyway, why all of a sudden you have such a keen interest in this? When Janis and I bailed you out, you certainly didn't seem to give a damn," he said in his evenly modulated tone. As long as Magrady had known the man, he could count on one hand when he'd heard him raise his voice. Nonetheless, he was forceful and compelling when he needed to be before a jury.

"It means something to me now. Do you know if there was, what do the cops call it, signs of a forced entry?"

"No, not that I remember. Seems Mr. Savoirfaire believed in his security. He had bars on his windows and subscribed to an alarm service. Whoever did the deed had been invited in, as I understand from my initial round of give and take with Stover. That's why he liked you for the deed, as he assumed you and the late street entrepreneur had business together."

That was somewhat different than what Stover had barked at him, but that just meant he was trying out a few theories to see which case jacket he could snugly fit on him, the motherfucker, Magrady groused. "If you can, Gordon, please check your notes today. That would be most useful."

"I will. But I must warn you not to interfere with an ongoing investigation et cetera, et cetera. You know the consequences for messing around in the LAPD's sandbox."

"I got that, counselor."

"Yeah, okay," he said without much conviction.

Magrady added, to put him at ease, "How the waves treating you?" Walters was in his fifties yet had still continued to pursue his avocation of surfing since his days as a teen growing up in Gardena—one of a select group of the Southland's black surfers. He had plenty of stories to tell of incidents where the mantra of 'locals only' being spouted at him by the stereotypical blue-eyed, blond-haired beach boys had double and triple meanings when he showed up to shred.

"Going to Tobago for this tourney next month."

"You ever run into Wakefield Nakano at these events?"

"Funny you should ask, I have a time or two. He's not a bad shredder."

"You two hang?"

"Not really. Why?"

"Can't find out the answers if I don't ask."

He chuckled deep in his throat. "Talk to you."

"Righteous." By the time he got back downtown, an orange glow tinged the bottom edge of the sky to the southeast. He and several other pedestrians gazed at this. Was it a fire or some new form of mutant smog?

"*Que lástima*," a heavyset woman balancing a plastic basket of freshly dried clothes on her head intoned, "*y no tengo carne para asar . . .*" They exchanged wan smiles and he walked on.

Passing by a corner liquor store, he heard on the radio newscast from inside that an as of yet unidentified aircraft had crashed in the Cleveland National Forest. The 130-mile swath of nature preserve created by President Teddy Roosevelt butted up against Riverside County with the bulk of its land covering the San Diego area. The exploding plane had ignited a spreading fire that several fire departments from the respective counties were responding to with all urgency. Magrady had a fond memory of being totally ripped on blow and beer while fishing at the reservoir there with some army buddies years ago.

At Urban Advocacy, Bonilla eyed him with a bemused look on her face as he entered. "You look worn out. Maybe you better take a nap, grandpa."

"I'm the one the Energizer Bunny comes to when he needs a boost."

"Look here," she said, indicating a desk with a cassette tape machine on it. "Ain't I good to you? It was in a desk we'd put in a back room. Carl had remembered seeing it there."

He was already over at the player and inserting the cassette tape he'd swiped from Chambers' sister. "Now we're getting somewhere." He depressed the play button and bent to listen. Bonilla came over too.

First there was a female voice saying, "Test, test," then she blew into the microphone. This was followed by a measure of silence on the tape when finally a male voice said, "It's quite remarkable, actually." Wind buffeted the mic.

The woman asked, "So who was Talmock, Professor Langston?"

"Well, you see," he began, clearing his throat. "The Chumash had what we might call a sect of craftsmen. These were men who passed on their skills at making and waterproofing the canoes, the various uses of whale blubber, preserving hides and so forth to their sons and so on. But they kept their methods close to the vest as it were."

"Meaning they didn't share their knowledge with the rest of the tribe?"

"Correct. Obviously a way to control the flow of information and to exalt their positions. Therefore their skills would always be in demand because not everyone had purchase of same. Which as we know is unusual for American Indians. More like Old World guild members," he noted. "Also the Chumash had female chiefs."

"How advanced for them," the woman said, and you could tell she was smiling.

Magrady clicked the tape off. "Great, a history lesson."

"Quiet. Let's keep listening." Bonilla put the machine back on.

More was said about the lifestyles of the Chumash, the Indian tribe that once inhabited the California coast, inland to a degree, and out into the Channel Islands. The Q&A wound back to Talmock.

"He was quite something," Professor Langston was saying, "both shaman and chief. He was said to have led a village of some five thousand people, a town really. Very unusual, for at the most their villages were no more than one thousand people and even that is something when you think about it. He seems to have openly had a wife and several concubines as well."

"The Mayor Villaraigosa of his day," Magrady cracked.

Bonilla shushed him.

There was more conversation. The woman said at one point, "So finding Talmock's mummified head is remarkable as you pointed out."

"Indeed, as the Chumash did not practice mummification of their dead, though we know the Aztecs did."

"Bolstering the speculation that Talmock possessed knowledge from other regions," the woman added. "Lending support to the thesis he was both chief and shaman."

Langston made a contemplative sound. "And of course there's the symbolism of Talmock's head. That is to say, there are those who would ascribe such properties."

"How do you mean?" the woman asked.

"Well, say like the Centurion Longinus' spear, said to have pierced Jesus' side at his crucifixion."

"The Spear of Destiny," the woman said.

"Yes. Or Poseidon's trident. Objects that imbue certain power and beliefs. In some cases faith, and in some cases magic I guess we'd have to say. And when it's a hand or head of a magical being, you can imagine how some can get quite excited." He chuckled dryly.

Magrady and Bonilla exchanged quizzical looks.

"So Floyd wants the head back because it will cure him," Bonilla opined, stopping the tape.

Magrady remained stonefaced.

"That was a joke, son."

"Maybe it ain't to Floyd." He flashbacked to moaning and bleeding soldiers, their wounds superglued together, taking drags on heroin-laced cigarettes and mumbling prayers for evac in the aftermath of VC Bouncing Betties exploding, severing limbs and ligaments. These were mines that when triggered shot up about three or four feet in the air then went off, their payload of scream-ing shrapnel ripping through bodies like buckshot through tissue paper. Too many times this was not due to a patrol not finding the mine, but to improperly crimping the thing. That meant squeez-ing the blasting cap and the fuse together just so as you disarmed the device. But invariably some junior officer fresh from asshole school was barking from a safe distance away about hurrying up, like defusing a bomb was as easy as ordering a pizza.

"He might truly see this as a way to walk again, Janis," he said seriously. Chambers had been crippled in an industrial accident, not the war, but the desire to walk again, to be whole physically was as much as the drive to be whole psychologically, Magrady concluded.

Momentarily she looked chagrined for belittling what might be their friend's goal but then brightened. "Or he wants to sell the head for money." A selfish reason was okay to deride.

"To who?"

She lifted a shoulder. "Talmock's head's gotta be worth something to a university or a collector. These kind of people pay big money for a baseball card with Ted Williams picking his nose on it so there must be a market for something like this artifact."

Magrady wondered if his head would ever become an ar-tifact . . . when he croaked homeless crack zombies would use a rusty hacksaw to remove it from his body and place it in a clear plastic box with a light inside of his hollowed out skull. They'd use his noggin as a nightlight to find discarded crack pipes containing minute residues of the enslaving rock. "His sister's office is over at USC, that policy project of SubbaKhan's." He stopped himself before admitting to her it was from that office he'd swiped the cassette tape. He didn't think she would object but if she didn't ask, he didn't have to tell.

Bonilla said, "She takes this gig to snatch the head back?"

"Hell if I know."

"Okay, so where's the head now?" She then added before he could respond, "Savoirfaire gets killed 'cause he had it?"

"What the hell would he have been doing with it, Janis? He wouldn't know it was valuable."

"What if he was holding it for ransom?"

Magrady considered this. "But Floyd came to me to get that clown to back off."

"Because Floyd had borrowed money from him. At least that's what he made it seem to us."

"Yeah . . ."

"But what if it wasn't?" Bonilla countered. "He put you against Savoirfaire to put him on you. Maybe he was going to slip it to him where to find you after you locked horns as he came after you, Floyd would burglarize his house to get the head back."

"I'm pretty sure being a paraplegic cuts down on your breaking and entering opportunities, Janis."

"He had help, butthead." She playfully socked him. "His sis."

"Come on, she's got this square job."

"But she could be working on the inside." She snapped her fingers, getting animated. "What if SubbaKhan has the head?" She stood up, pacing about. "Nakano has a private art gallery up in Malibu. Invitation only. We should go up there and see if the head is on display."

Magrady chuckled. "They ain't hardly going to let you in there, Mother Jones."

"How about your sorry self? Shit."

"Here's what I think," not deigning to acknowledge her dig, "Floyd needed me to get Savoirfaire off his ass 'cause he was going after the head and knew if homeboy was on him he might mess that up or take it from him once he stole it back."

She held up an index finger. "You're saying Floyd is after someone else who has the head?"

"Yeah, the guy who found it. Assuming it was a construction worker or laborer on the Emerald Shoals site. When did it break ground?"

"Two and a half years ago," she answered. "But you don't know who that is. And if he had it once, then say he turned it in to SubbaKhan, how'd he get it back?"

"What if he didn't turn it in? Could be he kept it and showed it to Floyd." Then it occurred to him. "He could be the sister's boyfriend. Only he'd said 'they' didn't know what they had."

"It could still mean he was referring to the sister and the boyfriend or maybe the boyfriend and a buddy."

A charge surged through Magrady. He felt as if the door was finally creaking open, if only a sliver. "I need to find the sister. Let me use the phone, will you?"

Bonilla checked her watch. "Go ahead, McGarrett. I need to get going anyway." She went to her desk to retrieve her messenger bag. As she slung it over her shoulder she asked, "You crashing at my crib tonight? Or are you and one of your GILFs shacking up?"

"It better be your place if you don't mind."

"Okay, playboy." She tossed him a key. "I had this cut just in case." She shook her index finger at him. "But don't you be bringing your ninety-year-old hoochies over there. I run a respectable house."

"Thanks, Janis. You're, you know . . . " he let it end there, suddenly self-conscious that they were in a public space.

She grinned. "Yeah, whatever." She left and he played more of the tape.

"Well, there's little evidence of that," the professor said hesitantly after the interviewer asked would Talmock have encouraged human sacrifice. "There's certainly no lore of the Chumash practicing such," he went on. "Though I'll grant you, if he was Aztec, he might well have tried to introduce this notion among the craft sect. But I'm sure he wouldn't have found converts given what we know of the ways of these coastal American Indians."

This speculation was dropped and there was further discussion about Talmock, who was said to have lived a long life, and to have taken several times what could be called spirit journeys into what is now San Bernardino County. Magrady listened awhile longer then turned the interview off. He then made a few calls on Bonilla's office phone, including leaving a message for Shane Redding at LRS, who was supposed to talk with Floyd's sister Sally. He was certain she'd want a meeting with him, given she knew he had the tape and had to figure he'd have played it by now.

Sitting at Bonilla's desk, he finally took the letter out from his ex-wife Claudelia. He looked at it for a few moments, knowing once he read it he couldn't ignore its message. He prayed it wasn't about their daughter or son, the latter he hadn't seen or heard from in more than seven years. He opened it and unfolded the single lined sheet. The letter was in that neat and precise handwriting of hers and informed him, after hoping this found him in good spirits, that she was undergoing chemo treatments for thyroid cancer. Her prognosis was good but she wanted him to know in case her treatment didn't go as expected.

He re-read the letter then folded it up and slipped it back into the envelope. She hadn't included a phone number to contact her but Magrady had expected she wouldn't. She hadn't sent this so he would come see her. This was about him reconnecting with the other members of his family.

Magrady folded the whole of it in half again and put it in his pocket. He did have his daughter's phone number and it seemed this was the time to call her. He tried dialing her number from memory but screwed up the sequence. He got his wallet out and found the slip of paper he'd written it on and tried again.

"Hi, this is the home of Evelyn, Cass, and Esther," a girl's voice said cheerily on the phone's recording. She giggled and he heard the whisper of an adult urging her on. "We're not here right now but please leave your message. Okay?" The beep followed and he spoke.

"Esther, this," he began haltingly and started over, "Esther, this is your father. I received the news about your mother and would like you to call me when you have a chance. This is the cell number of a friend of mine and she'll get your message to me. I'd like to see you and the children. Thanks."

He nearly said "Sorry," his regret making him queasy from his past failures as a father and husband. Quietly he cradled the handset, glad that no one was paying attention to him—or at least pretending not to. He was about to get back in the streets when Bonilla's phone rang. He ignored the ringing assuming it was for his friend and he used the restroom.

"Hey, Magrady," a voice said after a knock on the door to the toilet. "You in there?"

"Yeah?"

"Janis called in for you. Said hit her back on her cell."

"Thanks." He finished and returned the call.

"Shane told me she'd left two messages for Sally but hadn't heard back from her," Bonilla said over the phone. "Only she just heard from her and she was all worked about what was your story, how did you know her brother and all your 411."

"Good to see I rattled her after my dance with her brother. What else did she say?"

"Shane says Sally will only meet with you at the LRS offices. The implication being she wants lawyers around in case you try some shit."

Magrady snorted. "I'll ask Shane to let her know it's with her and Floyd or it's no go."

"Cool by me."

After he related his counter-demand to Redding, Magrady left Urban Advocacy and walked about, heading into the heart of downtown. He sifted through his emotions about his ex-wife's illness. Their romance was long ago tossed upon the junk heap of lost love but they had produced two children and even, if only for a time, a life together. The two-car garage and fondue party bit had gone to shit because of him so it wasn't like he held animosity toward her for running away from the drunk, high, irresponsible asshole he'd become back then.

Yeah, like he was a prince nowadays.

A sadness descended on him like a shroud and he sagged against a wall, feeling as if he were being sucked into a quicksand of despair he had little energy to struggle against. He wanted a drink or a joint, anything to escape the feeling. Any excuse would do to get high and forgetful.

He remained immobilized and uncertain for several minutes until a female voice said, "Mister, you want Gucci or Louis Vee? Got good Louis Vee, my brother."

Magrady looked over at a small woman of unidentifiable ethnicity with long garish nails, neon eyeliner, and piled-high black hair, her ample hips stuffed into too-tight satin peddle pushers. He blinked at her as if she or he had just arrived from an uncharted island as she swept a hand toward her knockoff designer-label luggage. He then realized he'd walked down to Broadway adrift in his self-pity and was leaning against the outside of the woman's cut-rate travel bags and electronic appliance emporium. This was socked into one of the retail slots on the ground floor of what had been the Tower movie theater. A *Los Tigres del Norte* song, "*Mi Lamento*," swooned from a tinny speaker.

"How about Hermès for your girl?" She cheerfully dangled several purses aloft to entice him.

Magrady wiped tears from his face and offered her a shaky smile as he moved away. The Spanish lyrics of the melancholy ballad fading out until it was a ghost sound filtered among the din of the busy street with various shopkeepers standing in front of their stores or stalls hawking wares from supposed iPhones that looked more like '80s-era calculators to the latest films barely released to the cineplexes on bootleg DVDs.

Blaring from the Cinco-Cinco discount electronics shop was the daytime local news on portable HD TVs. Field reporters were broadcasting from the Emerald Shoals site, construction going on behind them as they announced the upcoming opening of the complex, even with some of the facility not yet completed. The mayor, the head of the Central Cities Community Redevelopment Agency and various celebs were slated to be on hand to usher in this shiny symbol of the new downtown. A downtown for urban pioneers and those who could appreciate the fresh sushi bar in the Disneyland of Ralph's market dominating a corner of 9th Street. What, Magrady reflected dryly, low-wage workers couldn't push up on some yellowtail and avocado? No lattes for the homeless?

He walked to the Emerald Shoals and its office on site. "Is Chad Talbot available?" he asked the pleasant young woman behind the front counter.

"Is this business?" she asked neutrally, taking in Magrady's workmanlike appearance.

"Personal. But I can leave a message."

"Hold on," she said and she put two fingers to her ear like Uhuru in the original Star Trek. He hadn't noticed initially due to her long hair, but there was a Bluetooth in her ear. With her free hand she tapped on her keypad. She reached Talbot, Angie Baine's son.

"There's a gentleman here to see you, Chad." She looked over at Magrady and he told her his name. "Okay. Good." She severed the call. "He'll be right out."

"Thanks." Shortly Talbot came through a side door. It occurred to Magrady he hadn't seen the younger man in almost as long as he'd seen his own son. Then he was a chunky, scheming doper with long straggly hair and yellow eyes like a wolf's. The man before him was still stocky but now in a muscular way, military short hair and clear complexion. He wore black trousers and a grey blazer with the SubbaKhan logo on the breast pocket.

"Good to see you, man." He put out a hand and Magrady shook it. "Come on, let's go in the lunch room." He followed him through the door and along a hallway lined with framed photo prints of pro football players and singers. "I hear you and Mom are back together."

"Kinda, I guess."

Talbot grinned at him. "I know. She can be a handful." They came to the lunch room which had various types of high tech vending machines ranging from one that dispensed fresh vegetables, instant noodles and even one that cooked and delivered a nine-inch pizza.

"It's on me," Talbot said.

"Thanks." Magrady settled for a smoked turkey and pesto wrap and cranberry juice while Talbot had an egg salad sandwich with gouda and bottled water. There were construction workers and others in business attire also eating in the spacious area. The two sat at a table near an open exit doorway.

Talbot had some of his sandwich. "You came to see me about Luke? 'Cause I paid my mom back that thirty bucks in case you came to collect. Still getting used to budgeting."

That was how he must have found out about the two of them seeing each other again.

"No, that is, you've heard from him?"

"About four or five months ago. He's in New York. Involved in some kind of nightclub if I'm not mistaken."

"He called you?"

Talbot laughed easily then regarded Magrady. "He did. But I told him I'd gotten myself together with the help of Shera, that's my old lady. She's a Buddhist and believes in balance and harmony and she's certainly helped me in seeking mine."

"I can see that," Magrady said sincerely. "What did Luke want?"

"You'll have to talk to him about that." He smiled cryptically.

He wasn't going to push it. He probably wasn't ready for the answer. Magrady changed direction. "Actually, Chad, I'd come to see if you'd heard anything about a mummified head belonging to a Native American shaman named Talmock."

He stopped mid-bite. "You're serious?"

"Yes. Apparently the head was dug up at this site."

Talbot shook his head. "I haven't heard anybody talking about that. But I've only been here a little less than a year. Could have been discovered before my time when they broke ground. I'll ask around. What's this about?"

He told him an encapsulated version of events, leaving out his speculation that Chambers and his sister planned to rob this head from whomever had it.

Talbot made a low whistle. "Trippy."

Magrady chuckled. "What can I say?" They ate in silence, then, "I think your mom's real pleased with how you've turned out."

"I'm still on the journey. How're things with you?"

"Trying to keep my hand in."

Talbot chewed thoughtfully.

"Luke say anything else?" Magrady asked.

"He also asked about a couple of mutual friends, that sort of thing." He made a gesture with his hand. "You know Luke."

Magrady nodded, wondering if he did. They finished their food and he said, "I appreciate you seeing me, Chad. And very glad to see you're . . . on your journey."

The younger man was on his feet. "You want to take a quick tour?"

"That's okay. I'll be dazzled by the gleam when it opens like the rest of the suckers." He also stood and briefly clapped

Talbot on the back. "Though I wouldn't turn down a ticket or two to a Barons game now and then if you could swing it."

"Bet. I'll walk you out." They took a different route that let Magrady out on a side entrance. They shook hands again. "Good to see you too. And I hope your search is rewarding."

From there Magrady wound back to the edges of Skid Row. As he cut through an alley, more or less on his way to see Angie Baine—partly to tell her how impressed he was with her son now, and partly to take another look through Floyd Chambers' stuff—a car turned into the other end of the alley and started to pick up speed as it came at him. It was that god-damn Scion with Elmore at the wheel.

Magrady kicked some busted up wooden crates toward the car's grill. This had zero effect in slowing the vehicle. He turned and ran to get the hell out of there and saw a pile of bulging plastic trash bags next to a doorway. He lurched forward and grabbed the bags as the Scion bore down on him. Moving again, he flung the bags over his shoulder. Risking a quick glance around, he saw the exploding bags splatter all manner of slimy human detritus including rotting food across the windshield. This impaired Elmore's vision and turning on his wipers smeared the mess more. He slowed but he kept the car going straight and unswerving. Why shouldn't he? He knew where his target was.

V

SCARED, HE LOST HIS BALANCE as fear tripped him up like one of those nubile babes in cutoffs stumbling through the woods in a *Hills Have Eyes* movie. Magrady scooted forward on all fours, crashing into a dumpster. He scampered to the far end of it and using his shoulder shoved the other end of the dumpster crook-edly into the alleyway. The Scion's bumper grazed the edge and Elmore, still not seeing clearly, instinctively reacted by twisting the wheel. The car veered into the wall opposite, tearing up the front fender.

"Motherfuckah," Elmore swore, quietly, righting the car and skidding to a stop.

Magrady grimaced as he got on his feet, having wrenched his back pushing the dumpster. He looked around for something to hit the younger man with but would have to rely on his fists. Rather than wait for the attack, he rushed forward as the other man got clear of his car.

"I told you to stay the fuck out of my business, old man." Elmore socked Magrady in the gut and he doubled over. He moaned but would be goddamned if he was going to let this rooty-poot get the best of him that easy. He got his arms around the other's waist and driving his legs, as Elmore pounded his back, tumbled them against the Scion. They then slid to the ground, grappling like kids in a schoolyard brawl.

"Get the fuck off me, you decrepit goat," Elmore said, trying to nail Magrady with a right to his jaw.

The vet slipped the blow and got his hands around Elmore's neck and choked.

"That's enough," a voice declared over them, followed by the rapid crack of a baton along his shoulder blades and the base of his neck. Stunned and winded, Magrady let go and tried to get up. Elmore took this as an opportunity to exact damage and kneed Magrady in the groin.

As tears welled in his eyes and his lax body lay between the wall and the Scion, Magrady heard Elmore hollering. He got an eye open and saw the Taser dart sticking in the younger man's chest and he smiled wickedly. If he could, he would have peed on him to spark his ass up more.

Magrady rolled over onto his back and the officer placed a foot on his chest, his nine aimed at his nose.

"Don't fuckin' blink," the cop ordered. He called in the incident on the radio clipped to his shirt then ordered, "Both of you on your faces, now."

They did so, with Magrady's face lying on the back of Elmore's calf. They were both secured with plastic restraints then told to sit against the wall, clear of the Scion.

Magrady said, "I need some medical attention, officer." His face and upper body were going numb and he ached from his spine to his toes.

"Uh-huh," he said in that noncommittal way cops

answered perps. He'd dug out their wallets from their back pockets and was busying himself looking at their IDs. He wore a bike helmet and shades and had come up on them on his T3. These weren't Segways, as they had three wheels for better balance and mobility. The things looked more like a kid's futuristic electric scooter only there was a platform the officer stood upon, holding onto a vertical handle. Magrady had seen several of them being used by the cops patrolling the downtown area.

"How you feelin', champ?" Magrady said to bother Elmore. He was a few feet from him, his head down and breathing shallowly.

"Shut up," the cop, a youngish Asian man with planed shoulders, commanded.

A lanky bicycle cop peddled up. "Need a hand?" he asked.

"Sure, Dave, thanks," the other one replied. The two separated the prisoners and interrogated them briefly. Magrady coughed up blood at one point.

"Hope you drown, bitch," Elmore Jinks snickered.

The two officers were conferring when a cruiser came on the scene piloted by a sergeant. After parking, she talked to her officers then walked over to Magrady.

"You said you want a doctor?" she asked. Her dark green eyes probed his face and form. She looked closely at his scalp. There was a crimson wetness in his hair.

"I'm hurt," he said, meeting her gaze. He shifted uncomfortably.

There had been several recent incidents of hospitals dumping indigent patients on Skid Row, a couple of times caught on cell phone video—once with an LAPD patrol car going past. Added to that, a homeless woman had bled out three weeks ago after being stabbed and somehow getting into the secure lobby of a converted loft but being unable to summon anyone even though she buzzed several apartments. This story made the local news, and a guest op-ed in the *L.A. Times* by a homeless advocate posed the obvious question: would this woman have been ignored if she wore Uggs and had been accosted walking her Chihuahua?

The sergeant had no desire to be in a position to explain to the brass why an AARPer had died from an untreated head injury or sepsis under her watch. Magrady was transported to the thirteenth floor of County USC, the jail ward where, the lore goes, Magrady recalled, in the '50s junkie jazz saxman Stan Getz was cooling on the thirteenth floor while his wife gave birth right below him. Getz had been arrested for attempting to heist a pharmacy to get his morphine fix.

The jail ward was still housed in the old structure off Mission Road. The facility was now partly empty due to the newer county hospital opening nearby. Though this was also the grounds of the coroner where the bodies were kept and if need be, dissected. For prisoners, there was the tradition of iron beds and leg shackles. A doctor had seen to him briefly. Into the room came a tall female nurse with serious calves, veined forearms and her blonde hair in a long braid, who sternly and competently tended to the aching Magrady.

"Rest," she commanded and made a once around the room to check on the others under her charge. Everyone was silent, there was no sound save the quiet scuff of her rubber soled orthopedics across the worn linoleum. That changed as soon as uber-Heidi stepped out through the secured door.

"Fly me to the moon," a tatted and buffed *vato* in the bed on one side of Magrady suddenly crooned in a pretty fair imitation of Sinatra. He actually wasn't too bad, especially as he helped drown out the sounds of the man in the bed on the other side of him.

This one, bald but also in his twenties, had a leg and arm in casts and groaned and moaned. "Please help me," he pleaded, "I can't go back in there. He's gonna have his way with me. Oh, please Great Umagoomah, I just can't go."

In a bed set closer to the door, an older, heavier man with curly grey and white hair lay. He talked to himself, doing his multiplication tables. He kept going higher in value, not once making a mistake as far as Magrady could tell. The fifth bed's occupant, this one under the barred window, lay still on his stomach, snoring.

The nurse had poked Magrady with an IV drip of some sort of painkiller that mellowed him out like when he used to in-dulge and float away on Hendrix's "Purple Haze" and Funkadelic's

"Maggot Brain." He put an arm across his eyes and dozed, the looping cacophony of his fellow inmates an infirmary lullaby.

"Dreaming of me?" a harsh voice said, disrupting his reverie.

"Always, captain." Magrady was loath to remove his arm but did so. The real world had to be confronted. Stover hovered near him, enjoying the sight of the former non-com laid up.

"So what's the deal with you and Elmore Jinks?" the cop asked, standing over the vet.

Magrady considered lying but he figured he'd get more joy out of telling him the truth, as it demonstrated his defiance. He used the control to raise the top half of the bed. "I was looking for Floyd Chambers and those two jacked me in a bar in Inglewood."

"Thought you said you didn't know Savoirfaire."

"Still didn't, except for the time we had our tête-à-tête."

"You find Chambers?"

"Yeah, but lost him again." That was more or less accurate.

Stover chuckled. "I guess this Peter Gunn thing ain't your bag, Magrady."

"Seems that way."

"Why'd Jinks try to park his car on your chest?"

"What he say?"

Stover examined him. "He didn't."

Magrady told him about his run-in with Elmore Jinks' partner Boo Boo, and him being with Chambers.

"Why you all so hot and bothered to find Chambers?"

"Do you think he killed Savoirfaire?"

Stover smiled thinly. "We got you for that, homey."

"You honestly believe the DA will press that case against me?"

"I know you to be capable of fatal indiscretions, Magrady."

"You gotta get off that merry-go-round, Stover."

He pointed at him. "Or you got away with something belonging to Savoirfaire after you iced him and the Rover Boys want it. Maybe Chambers was in on it with you, set Savoirfaire up for you to bash his head in."

"Believe what you like, Captain. But Jinks came at me and you need to do your job and put his ass away."

"Don't you worry about how I do my job, sport."

Stover departed and Magrady was treated to a rendition of "Danke Schoen" from the Singing Vato. There was a TV playing mutely high up in one corner of the room. On it was a newscast about the fire that had consumed several thousand acres in Cleveland National Forest. On screen at one point was an artist's rendition of a space-age-looking jet that, the crawl informed Magrady, was rumored to have gone down in the forest.

Their dinners arrived, pushed in by an athletically-built light-skinned African American orderly named Rekon according to his name tag.

"They call you that because you were in the service?" Magrady asked him, pointing at his pin. The orderly pushed his plate of roast beef and cream corn into place. The knuckles on the orderly's hands were misshaped from repeated impact.

"It's my fighting name," he said in a surprisingly gentle voice. "Short for Rekonso."

Magrady frowned. "You're not a boxer. The bruises on your hands are wrong for that. You don't get that from wearing the heavy gloves."

Rekon raised an eyebrow, nodding. "Mixed martial arts, old school."

"Brutal," Magrady lamented.

"Me and my old lady are pursuing it. She's got a bout down in Maywood this Saturday."

"I guess that keeps the arguments to a minimum at home."

He laughed. "So you try and rob somebody?"

"Just trying to help a friend."

"Right, right," the other one said, having heard all manner of inmates' excuses for winding up in the hospital jail ward. He finished his chore and departed.

After sunset the Asgardian nurse returned and Magrady asked her about making a phone call.

"You're being sent to central booking tomorrow and you can make it there," she said tersely as she changed his IV.

"I need to talk to my lawyer. He doesn't know I'm here."

"He will," she said, giving him a pat on the arm as she moved off.

Magrady was inclined to take his frustration out on her but knew she was practiced in the art of deflection when it came to hard luck prisoners. Certainly if he really got insistent, Rekon would be summoned double-quick and show him why his knuckles looked like they did. But he felt adrift, deprived of his freedom and prevented from carrying out his duties. Duties? To whom? To himself, the eternal search for the greater truth? Bullshit. Maybe to the magical mummified head of Talmock. Sure, why not?

The sound was now up on the TV and another news report was on about the fire. It was now nearly forty percent contained. Switching from a live feed with a fire captain at the scene, the report then played a previously taped snippet with an Air Force spokesman from their PR office who would neither confirm nor deny the persistent rumors that an experimental aircraft, the Serpent's Wing, had crashed in the forest.

"I can't speculate on that at this juncture," the tense-jawed spokesmen said in answer to a reporter's question that, if the plane did go down, was terrorism suspected.

That night in the dark, Magrady lay in bed on his back, imagining some miscreant had used Talmock's head to bring down the experimental jet and that Boo Boo and Elmore Jinks wanted it to fix horse races and mesmerize large-breasted women to do their lascivious bidding. Around two in the morning he awoke and removed the intravenous drip from his arm. Pain would keep him more on edge. He felt he was going to need all his resources soon.

VI

MAGRADY'S LEG IRON CLANKED as he walked from the bathroom back to his bed. Before he could climb back in, the lock turned and two Sheriff's deputies entered. One was what you'd expect of a sumabitch that had to corral the Southland's often querulous inmate population. He was big, muscularly wide in the upper body and at least six-five. The eyes in that flat bronze Olmec face turned this way and that, partially lit by the pale fluorescents in the hallway behind him. He absorbed data, assessing the bullshit quotient and possible threat the hospitalized prisoners in the room might have posed—if the rest had been awake. The sun wouldn't be up for another twenty minutes or so, but a man closer to collecting Social Security than he liked to admit had a prostate operating on its own clock.

"Aravilla," the considerable one said over the sounds of slumber. He didn't wait for an answer and then announced, "Magrady." He again seemed disinterested in a response as he stepped back and his more normal proportioned companion came forward.

This one had red hair going grey at the sides and freckles along his forearms. "This ain't *American Idol*, ladies. No sense being coy, it won't earn you more points. Let's go. You're keeping me from my breakfast burrito," he cracked.

"Magrady, Aravilla, up and ready." The ancient-faced one turned on the lights amid throat clearing and farting. His partner tossed a folded up jailhouse orange overall to Magrady who'd held up his hand.

"Lemme see your tag," The redhead demanded, indicating with his fingers for the vet to come toward him. He did and showed him the plastic ID bracelet around his wrist. He then unshackled Magrady, tossing the ankle collar onto the older man's hospital bed. The chain attached to the collar had its other end fastened to a welded ring in the floor, the length of which allowed the wearer movement about the room.

"We going to Central?" the Singing Vato asked, sitting up, blinking and yawning.

"You Aravilla?"

"Yeah."

The deputy pitched the crooner the other coverall and checked to make sure he was the intended. Aravilla got into his getup after getting free of his leg chain as Magrady fastened his coveralls. Then the two were handcuffed with a thinner chain reattached to both ankles and their wrists, then linked to each other. In this way Magrady and the Singing Vato were marched out in line, the red haired deputy in front and the larger one behind them. His knobby, veined hand rested casually on the butt of his pistol. All through this preparation, the other prisoners had watched them go save the one who'd been doing his multiplication tables. He remained in bed, seemingly asleep and oblivious.

The two were taken down in an elevator to a prisoner transport van at a loading dock, and driven out onto Mission Road.

Magrady and Aravilla exchanged a look. The van wasn't heading south toward downtown and the central jail. The van took the ramp onto the 10 freeway, west.

"Where we headed, chief?" Aravilla asked the back of the deputies' heads through the heavy wire mesh between them and the front of the van. There was no answer, and no other prisoners were in the back. "Motherfuck," Aravilla swore, impotently jerking his chains in frustration. The two were sitting opposite one another, secured to a steel loop bolted to the floor.

Magrady sat back and tried not to fixate on the drama. Stover was having him buried in the system. Their paperwork would go missing, purposely misfiled and not in the proper computer files. So friends or relatives searching for them among the arrestees at Central or the Twin Towers wouldn't find them too easily.

"Who'd you piss off?" Magrady asked Aravilla.

"This punk ass over at Rampart. A real prick sergeant who's been bangin' my cousin."

"I'm guessing you've made your displeasure known to him."

"Indeed," the other man said, sighing. "They're gonna stick us somewhere out in the boonies where no one can find us." He jerked on his chains again. "Man, I had an audition to get to tomorrow. This is really fucked up."

It turned out that Aravilla was part of a talent agency geared toward helping ex-gangbangers get roles in TV shows and movies. He'd been up for a part in a cable three-parter in which the criminals and cops sang pop tunes and social commentary numbers à la Brecht and Weill or Springsteen, reflecting on their deeds. He was looking forward to playing the part of a mercurial character nicknamed the Chairman, hence his getting the Sinatra imitation down. But he had a run-in with the sergeant at a neighborhood eatery in Boyle Heights. The cop was off duty and, according to Flores, had goaded him about banging the shit out of his favorite aunt's youngest daughter.

Such unflattering comments led to fists flying and Aravilla wound up getting pounded several times in the kidney by the officer's shoe. With blood in his urine, he'd earned an overnight stay in the jail ward. In hindsight this was less about seeing to his injuries, but a way to disappear the struggling song man.

The van made good time on the freeway as this was before the morning crush. From the 10 they segued onto the 405 North and hit a pocket of resistance past the Getty Center before dropping down through the Sepulveda Pass. The reason for the delay was a camouflaged Army Humvee that rear-ended by a civilian Hummer, a smaller H3, in the middle lane. Several service men and a woman had exited the Army vehicle and were discussing matters with a middle-aged woman in a fur coat, the driver of the Hummer. This Magrady took in as they rolled past.

The large deputy, who drove, said something to his partner and the other one snickered. He took a look back at the prisoners, a leer fading on his face. "Just relax, fellas. I can almost taste that burrito."

"Good for you," Magrady said.

"Careful, pops, you might want to save your strength."

Redhead pointed a finger at him and turned back around. "You got a long day ahead of you."

"That right?" Magrady challenged.

Aravilla made a disapproving frown at him.

Eventually the prisoners were deposited at the Van Nuys County jail facility, part of a sprawling complex that included an LAPD division and nearby courthouse. They were placed in a holding cell with other arrestees, including an atypical white, tanned, suburban-looking man in tasseled loafers and suede sport coat. He did his best to remain in a corner, seemingly trying to will himself invisible to the rest. Naturally this had the opposite result.

"The fuck, man," a beer gut hanging, bearded individual said as he gazed mercilessly at the casually dressed inmate. "They bust you for trying to pick up a prostitute, something like that?" he demanded. No response. "What? You deaf, bitch? I got something to open up your ears."

The object of his twisted desire tried to get smaller.

"They didn't treat Britney like this," a Marilyn Manson copycat said to a deputy who walked by the bars, reading something on a clipboard. The pop singer had once reported to this jail for whatever infraction she'd committed that week. She'd come in a bright red wig and miniskirt as countless paparazzi snapped photos in hopes she'd do something bizarre in the continuing headline drama of her then public meltdown. Instead she just filled out her paperwork and was able to leave.

Yeah, Magrady lamented, they sure didn't treat Britney Spears like this.

Every minute that elapsed brought him no relief since he had no idea as to a time certain for release. He'd asked at one point to make a phone call but lacking money couldn't use the pay phone. Magrady considered hitting up the suburbanite for some quarters but given he hadn't said anything to defend him, he felt he didn't deserve to ask for the loan. But he got his chance after they'd been brought a lunch of grilled cheese sandwiches piled on a tray, just out of the microwave.

"Hey, my doctor says I can't let my blood sugar get too low," the one with the stomach said to the loafer wearer. He held out his hand for the other one to hand over his food.

"Look, just let me be."

Jelly belly jiggled his hand, waiting, entitled to receive his tribute.

Magrady orbited closer. "You're not that stupid, are you?"

He put squints on the vet. "Fuck off."

"I've got nowhere to go," Magrady said. It got quiet in the holding tank.

"I said step off, whiskers."

"Now you know damn well these fine deputies like to run an orderly jail. You want to cause a ruckus, that's one more charge laid on your head. Me," he hunched his shoulders, "I don't mind the extra days." He figured two or three blows from those meaty fists and he'd be back in the hospital ward, but he couldn't abide a bully. "See, I like the taste of ears," making a reference he'd go Mike Tyson on him.

Gut man took a step closer to Magrady who didn't blink nor back up. He was ready to plant his elbow in the man's Adam's apple.

Several beats, then, "My fine old lady's comin' to spring me. I don't have time for this shit."

That earned him a round of disappointed guffaws as the potential combatants separated—which in their tight, crowded space meant several inches. The middle class man continued to unwrap his sandwich and began eating. He glanced once at Magrady, wary to know what his intercessor wanted from him.

"I didn't ask for your help and I'm damn sure not giving you anything," he said over a mouthful.

"Sucker," Aravilla said to Magrady, smiling thinly.

Magrady ate slowly and tried to remember various passages from Jules Verne's *20,000 Leagues Under the Sea*. It was the first book he'd picked out on his own as a kid to read from the school library. Trying to conjure up those scenes, and that thrill of those word pictures in his head at that time, gave him something to do. Something to do for a while until that got boring. At eighteen past four he was imaging how his shoes had been manufactured when a deputy called for Aravilla.

The Singing Vato stuck out a fist to Magrady. "Stay up, home."

"You too, man," he said, giving the other one some pound. "I'll look for you in the movies."

"That's right."

The cell door was unlocked and he left, flanked by the pair that had brought them there. Magrady's stomach fluttered. Like him, Aravilla hadn't made a call to let anyone know where he was and there wasn't going to be a court hearing this late in the day. And he doubted a friend had found him.

Aravilla didn't look back, but hesitated as he was led through the doorway as those questions must have occurred to him as well. Forty minutes later, Magrady was called and he too was taken through the doorway by the happiness boys. The room they stood in contained two chairs and a mop leaning against the wall. Another door, with an electronic lock, was at the far end.

"Take that off," the red haired one said, handing Magrady a grocery bag containing his mushed clothes.

Magrady removed the overalls and put on his pants and shirt. He put a hand on his back pocket. "Where's my wallet?"

The two looked blankly at each other. "Wallet, you say," the heavyweight replied. "We don't know nothin' about that. It must have been taken at the hospital."

"Shitty security they got there," his tag team buddy said, clucking his tongue.

"This ain't right." The key to Bonilla's place was missing too. "How the hell am I supposed to get home?"

"You're a free man, sir." The walloper moved to the security door and punched in a combination. The door clicked open a sliver and he pushed it further out. "Best get going." His Olmec face was set like carved granite.

The other one gave Magrady a glazed look, and for the briefest of moments he wanted to smash that face, if only to get arrested and have a place to sleep tonight. No matter how uncomfortable the holding tank was and having to deal with the blowhard with the beer belly. But he knew better and walked out the door that they'd put Aravilla through less than an hour before. He was let out onto the side of the building and a passageway along a parking structure. The door closed behind him.

Fuckin' Stover. No money and no coat and it was getting cold. Magrady walked over to Van Nuys Boulevard and went south. He begged fifty cents at a gas station off a youngster riding a sweet 1200 cc Yamaha motorcycle. At a supermarket, he was awarded two dollars for helping an aging woman with dyed bright orange hair load her church van with various boxes of out-dated, but eatable food donated to their pantry.

"You sure you don't want me to help you get a bed tonight?" she asked Magrady. "I know several shelter operators in the area."

"That's okay, thanks. I'll be fine. I appreciate this." He waved at her and walked off. It was nighttime and he was frigid. Hustling money was one thing, but staying at a shelter would depress him even more as to how precarious his situation was. Nearing Burbank Boulevard he came upon a funky coffee shop and entered. An open mic session was happening. A chunky young woman with hot pink highlights in her hair was humorously recounting her time chained to an old oak to prevent it being bulldozed while desperately having to pee.

Magrady warmed up and managed not to spend his money. There were numerous people in the place and when the couple left, he sat in one of their chairs and pretended the half full cup before him had been his. He also carefully stole some tip money. He knew at least once this young woman in fur boots caught him but she smiled wanly in an understanding way. There was a working pay phone near the bathroom and Magrady tried a collect call to Janis Bonilla. But the operator couldn't put it through since he only got her recording.

Back in his seat he noticed one of those canvas bag type purses on a nearby ledge. Whoever it belonged to wasn't around at the moment. Magrady zoomed in on several bills haphazardly stuffed into it. A few bucks more and he could catch a bus back to his side of town. Just two lousy dollars. He was hungry as hell and cold and uncomfortable, but wanted to get home worse. He looked around and the storyteller with the bright hair who'd been rockin' the mic earlier glanced up from the text she was editing while sitting at a table. They exchanged half smiles and she resumed her work.

But Magrady knew she'd checked off the petty thief box in her head and would be aware if he reached for the money. His taking a risk for the ducats became moot as the owner of the bag, a curvaceous mixed-race young woman in hip huggers, returned.

A little past eleven the open mic session was over, and the coffee house was closing up. He tried a collect call again to Bonilla, but again no luck. As Magrady started to leave, he noticed a color flyer sticking out from underneath a saucer with a partially eaten piece of marble cake on it. Magrady ate the cake and grinned at the image on the leaflet as he pulled it loose. The slick advertised a local gallery, the Middle Eye, which had a show up about early California. The graphic was a photo of the floating mummified head identified as Talmock.

Magrady had expected the mystic to have his lips and eyelids sewn together and spiders crawling along straggly hair like some apparition out of an old EC Comics horror eight-pager. His lips were closed and the reptilian skin drawn tight across his protruding cheekbones. But the eye sockets were open and gems of some sort had replaced the orbs. Was this why Floyd and his sister wanted the head? For the jewels? But how much could they be worth? A few thousand at most. That didn't make any sense he reasoned. If Talmock had been buried with the jewels in his eye sockets, whoever unearthed the head would have snatched them. Down at the lower left in small letters the credits included a thank you to the Nakano Family Foundation. He took the flyer with him.

Energized by the new information, Magrady went in search of another pay phone but couldn't find one that worked. He had to take a dump and did his business in an alcove beside a nail salon set on a tiny strip mall. He used some thrown away fast food wrappers to clean himself. He wasn't embarrassed. This was a necessity, and like any other bereft person, he did his best to adapt to his present conditions.

He wanted to at least reach Ventura Boulevard because he knew how to get back downtown on Line 96. For this was the Valley and even more about mobility via private car than where he normally hung. So he walked. He soldiered up into the dark and the cold, putting one foot in front of the other.

Fuck Stover.

Fuck Boo Boo and Elmore.

Fuck 'em all.

Blowing on his fists, Magrady walked on, telling himself that each step brought him closer to a bed and sleep—even if he wasn't really sure where that would be. At the bus stop his frigid fingers were lanced with pins of cold in his pockets as he stamped back and forth behind the bus bench. Finally the bus came and he paid his fare and slumped in a seat in the rear, among four other passengers. There was heat and he unfroze.

One of the other passengers was a man about Magrady's age in polyester pants, a dirty corduroy sport coat, and a Bob Marley T-shirt. He mumbled algebra formulas to himself and laughed at his answers. Exhausted, Magrady half-slept till the bus got over the hill and turned to let them out on Hollywood Boulevard to transfer to the next bus. Magrady and a woman he took to be an office cleaner given her blue khakis and work shirt under her coat, waited.

The two exchanged quick nods as the Black Flame and the Dread Knight walked up, sharing a flask. The newcomers nuzzled each other. Each had on a jacket, and the Dread Knight's cape trailed below his car coat. He offered the booze to Magrady and the other woman. She declined but Magrady had a sip. His first drink in eight months. Damn, he missed the stuff.

"Hard day, huh?" the Dread Knight asked him, slipping his cowl off to reveal a ruggedly handsome face. Along the Boulevard, some who were looking to make their break in the Industry and in between waiting tables or selling cell phones, would dress as superhero or fairytale characters and prowl about, looking to swoop in and have their picture taken with the typical gawking tourist, whose kids invariably would be the ones to point at them and exclaim their character's name. Said costumed adventurer would then hit up their unsuspecting patron for a tip for their so-called service. Thus unlike the do-gooders they pretended to be, they would depart before a security guard or cop could run them off or bust them for panhandling.

"You know it," Magrady concurred.

The Black Flame, a good-sized woman in a straining

skimpy top, fired up a joint done up in a chocolate blunt wrap. Magrady was tempted but was determined to fall back into one vice at a time. He did have another sip and soon all four were passing the time with talk of no consequence. When the bus came they got on and sat in separate areas. But when the Black Flame and the Dread Knight got off on Western and Beverly, the man gave a half wave and Magrady returned the gesture. Through the bus windows, he watched the city go by in the early morning semi-dark.

Back downtown, out of perverse pride, he didn't go by Bonilla's or Angie Baine's place. Maybe he didn't want them to smell the liquor on his breath. He got down to the Nickel. He found some greasy and musty clothing tatters in a cardboard box. He gathered the remnants under an arm and went on. Magrady passed a grouping of twenty-somethings spilling out of an after-hours spot called Che's Barracks. They were lining up to get food from the Goro-Ga spicy sausage lunch truck. A pretty woman in a micro-mini bit into a chili dog as she weaved along the street with her two giggling female friends in their high heels. She gently bumped into Magrady.

"Hi," she said sweetly.

He grunted and kept walking.

"Hey," she said, "mister."

Magrady turned to see her silently offering him her food. She wore no makeup, probably sweating it off dancing all night he surmised. She smiled genuinely. Her friends glared at him with unfocused eyes.

"Thank you," he said quietly. They three didn't laugh behind his back as he walked on, finishing the chili dog. There were some chili fries in the bag too. He wiped his mouth on his found clothes when he was done. Then using the clothes the best he could like blankets, he slept under the Sixth Street Bridge with several others.

In his dream a one-eyed talking tiger like in the animated *Jungle Book* chased him through the dense Vietnamese undergrowth. The tiger said he was late for his dental appointment. He awoke at light with a hard-on and wanting a drink.

VII

DOMINGO AGUDIN POPPED THE TOP on the Aleve bottle and shook out two tablets. He placed one in his shirt pocket and downed the other one with his morning coffee. Overhead a plane glided along its flight path into nearby LAX, the rattle rising through his shoes barely registering as he sat at the kitchenette table. Living in a two-bedroom apartment in Lennox with his wife and two fast growing daughters—did Olga really need those new shoes so soon?—the concrete overlaps of the busy 105 and 405 Freeways casting shadows across the windows, you got used to a lot. But this week, as it had been for several weeks, he had no complaints, aches and stiff fingers notwithstanding.

He was doing dry wall on the rehab of yet another condo conversion. Did the *gabachos* never tire of their precious tiny balconies and all the just-so marble counters and what did they call it? Stressed surfaces. To make furniture look like it had been in use for some time. Yes, the stressed wood of the fireplaces and dinner tables also had to be just so—a phrase he'd heard the heavily perfumed realtor utter often. And if that wasn't enough, the owners of this building, given they were not exactly in a stylish neighborhood yet, were also giving away cars when you bought a condo. That is, they'd pay for your lease on a Mini Cooper for the first year if you paid the incredible price it cost you to buy one of their fancy boxes.

He made a face in the half-light. This crazy shit brought work, and work was always needed. No matter he couldn't afford to move his family into the place he was fixing up. The building he was now restoring had once been a hotel for the likes of fry cooks, housekeepers and those passing through with no present and no past. Then at some point it became some kind of halfway house. It was way down on Grand, near the DMV office and Exposition Boulevard, not in the already-fancy redone part of downtown L.A. Agudin knew the place had been a halfway house because some years ago he'd had a distant cousin, recently released from Corcoran and in some sort of drug program, wind up there. His mother had called him from Sinaloa and asked him to drive over there and see if there was anything he could do for this unknown relative.

Do for him? Agudin shook his head at the memory. There they were with an infant and a toddler, his wife working a part-time waitress job at a sports bar keeping hands off her ass and him getting day work standing outside the Home Depot. But it was his mother so he went. The cousin answered to his street name, Frog Boy, but damned if he could remember his actual one now. He was as he'd expected him to be, a sullen, the world-owes-me-a-living lump who blamed everybody else for his troubles. Agudin gave him ten dollars he could ill afford to give, got a grunt for a reply, and his good deed was done.

Two or three years after that, he got word that Frog Boy had been shot in the head trying to hold up a jewelry store in Albuquerque. Turns out the retired sheriff of the county was in there that day to purchase a diamond anklet for a new firecracker of a girlfriend. From what he understood, Frog Boy amazingly managed to run away, leaking blood. Whether Frog Boy lived or died, nobody in the family knew.

Washing out his cup, Agudin considered what the world brings you.. How the wheel always turns and how the episodes of your life always seem to come back around to you. The dream he'd had last night, was it an omen of what was to come? This one had stayed with him and hadn't blown away like smoke as most of his dreams usually did. The old head he'd dug up about a year ago working as a laborer on the Emerald Shoals project had floated to him as he walked along a dark street, bare trees with branches like icy fingers reaching for him as a steady wind blew.

He arrived at a particular house, names murmured on the wind but were indistinguishable to his ears. The door was nicely stressed he'd noted. He walked in and there, in what would be the living room, Frog Boy was stretched out on a stone slab atop several squat cactus plants. He stood over Frog Boy who was dressed like a pilot in the World War II movie he'd seen on TV late one night, *Twelve O'Clock High*. He looked okay, no head wound he could see, only he just lay there, seemingly unable to get up. But when Frog Boy talked some kind of nonsense came out of his mouth. That's when the head reappeared and translated Frog

Boy's words, reciting a recipe for making his *abuela's* enchiladas.

Gathering his tools and lunch, Agudin still regretted turning over the head but he didn't have a choice. He'd been part of the crew digging trenches for piping, and there it was. Somehow it hadn't been crushed as the grader had recently finished scraping away a layer of earth from the side of a rise. At first, seeing the face partially sticking out of the dirt in that hillside, Agudin figured a kid must have thrown his Halloween mask into the worksite. But he went over to it and with little effort pulled the Indian head free and stared at it.

By then a few of the others had noticed, and murmuring was going around the site about what he found. One guy, a welder, said it must have been a drug dealer who was chopped up after a deal gone bad. Another worker opined it seemed to him the head was probably older than that. As they gathered around him, Agudin's chance to hide his find and maybe sell it to a museum or a collector vanished. The foreman came over and took possession, thanking Agudin and telling everyone to get back to work.

A week later the big boss Wakefield Nakano showed up with a pretty photographer. The dirt had been brushed off and the head was in a safe box locked in the foreman's office. He and Nakano stood side by side, each having a hand under the glass case he'd put the head in, smiling goofy grins while photos were taken. Nakano also had him sign some paper about making sure that Agudin knew what he found on SubbaKhan property belonged to the company. What could he do? Refuse? Run away with the head? How far could he go and what would that get him but thrown in jail. He signed the goddamn paper.

The construction was stopped for a time as some college types and their students came to the site to do their special digging looking for more heads or pots or arrow tips, but nothing else was found. Agudin didn't see any extra money in his check and eventually when his part of the job was done, that was that. Though a few of the men, including Latinos, had joked with him about finding the head, calling him Tamale Raider, Indiana Mex and what have you.

Odd that after putting the mummy head out of his mind so he wouldn't be bitter, his wife had warned him, he had a dream about it and Frog Boy. He checked his watch. Whatever it meant, he concluded, that dry wall wasn't going to install itself, as his supervisor kept telling him and the crew. Agudin left for work.

∘ ∘ ∘

WAKEFIELD NAKANO RODE HIS horse Harbinger into Bixby Stadium in Long Beach. The freshly mown grass was a heady aroma for rider and beast. Bouncing slightly in the saddle, Nakano trotted the horse around some, letting her stretch her muscles. He graduated the mare into a gallop, then seamlessly went into his check and turn with the animal. He smiled, imagining the bump he was going to deliver against Caleb Anderson in the upcoming charity match. That bastard wasn't going to ride him off like he did in last year's match. Damn that grin-and-bear-it model-minority Asian shit. Nakano had a long memory.

He practiced some swings with his mallet on the new composition plastic ball that was going to be used on Saturday. The weight of the ball was regulated but each time some new version was introduced, you had to get the feel of the thing; how it spun, its response to being hit and particularly how that ball rolled once it contacted the turf after flight. He struck and moved, horse and rider leaning and surging forward, pulling back and making their turns and cuts cleanly. He came to a rest and wiped sweat off his face with his sleeve.

He then rode over to inspect the ad boards on the arena wall for the Cherry Barrel vineyard he'd invested in last spring. The label had been started by some friends from business school, some of whom had had successes as restaurateurs. He still wasn't too crazy about the logo. This was supposed to impart poshness, but maybe after all he was just a kid who grew up in the JA section of the Crenshaw District. Sitting on Harbinger, studying the sign, the damn words were too hard to read in that fru-fru script the designer had insisted on using. Still, if it sold it must be good, so he'd quit fixating on the lettering and wait for the year-end report.

His cell phone buzzed and after digging it out, Nakano answered. "Yes?"

"Wake," his assistant Alicia Sinnott began, "we're getting complications from the mayor's office."

Harbinger shook his mane and Nakano patted his corded neck as he talked. "What does he want?"

"His office has forwarded different language on the Housing Trust Fund section."

"Why is that a problem?"

She said flatly, "You should read it."

"Come on, Alicia," he laughed dryly, "I doubt he's calling for the sort of set-asides and punitive measures on developers that his one-time allies Urban Advocacy are calling for."

"You know him. He doesn't want to be seen as, well, flitting from one thing to the next."

"But he does," Nakano observed. Though he was certain SubbaKhan would pony up for his re-election bid, which was looming. The mayor had his drawbacks, but once he got on task, he got results. He was a hell of a negotiator, and shared a lot of the conglomerate's vision for remaking the city.

"He wants this to have some teeth," she said. "I think he finally figured out the report wasn't going to be the usual dull, academic exercise and he wants to make sure the Trust is seen as real."

They both were aware that the mayor had created rifts among the shaky alliance of grassroots activists, organized labor, and the boardroom denizens that had brought him to office. He'd been politically wounded for not having a comprehensive affordable housing strategy with the Trust Fund being a somewhat moribund proposal he'd grasped at, though it had been inherited from the previous administration. It was the mayor's people who shoehorned a section on the Trust Fund into the report the Central City Reclaiming Initiative that SubbaKhan underwrote was readying. The report offered a series of recommendations regarding sustainable living conditions, using the Emerald Shoals effort in the downtown area as a hub from which to build out.

"And the mayor needs to entice some of his detractors back to the fold." Nakano said to her.

Harbinger was getting restless standing still and Nakano started her in a circuit around the field to cool down properly.

"I'll be in to go over the rewrite then talk with him. I also want to schedule time to have another meting with our friends."

"Before the report comes out?" his assistant asked. Part of SubbaKhan's strategy was to use friendly press around the report as a way to blunt the ongoing attack from the coalition of community groups. The so-called united front was using the Environmental Impact Report's findings to slow the expansion anchored by the Shoals project. SubbaKhan was not opposed to these measures, but had to balance such concerns with reasonableness and profit margins. Too bad Urban Advocacy and its ilk didn't have the building trades perspective who were all about growth because it meant their members were working, buying new pickups and making those timely house payments.

Why the hell did Reagan bring down the Berlin Wall if not to symbolize the triumph of the free market Nakano groused inwardly. The historic televised speech of the Gipper at the Brandenburg Gate challenging Gorbachev had determined his course when Nakano was a kid. Wasn't it bad enough he had to learn Chinese for the sake of business? America had to hold on and he was for damn sure doing his part to get her back on her feet post the meltdown. He refocused.

"Just set it in motion, Alicia. It's all about good faith, isn't it?"

"Fine, fine," she drawled and hung up.

Nakano headed Harbinger back to the horse trailer hitched to his Range Rover. He couldn't help picturing himself as the laconic Gary Cooperesque cowpoke on his way to face down the owlhoots. After securing his horse, he looked out into the empty stands and saw a headless man in cotton pants and faded floral shirt and moccasins. He had one leg crossed over the other, arms folded, waiting.

"Yes," Nakano nodded solemnly at the seated Talmock. "I understand."

o o o

SATURDAY NIGHT AND FLOYD Chambers wheeled up to a plate glass window of the Middle Eye Gallery and looked in on the reception for the early California exhibit. The show had been up for more than a week, but this was the first time Professor Cyrus Langston had been able to attend. Prior to that the older gentleman, who got around well for a man in his late seventies, had been on an excavation in Kenya.

Tall women with legs that made Chambers lightheaded and dudes in black on black flitted about, laughing and talking and nibbling little cheeses from offered trays. Some stood before paintings or pieces of crumbling pots on pedestals pointing at them and nodding their heads at each other.

His sister casually looked from the mummified head on display in the gallery, and toward her brother. She betrayed nothing and moved on, sipping her champagne from a plastic flute like Tyra Banks regarding the skanks at a fashion review, Chambers imagined. He got set to do his part to steal Talmock's head.

Floyd Chambers wheeled into the Middle Eye Gallery and earned a nod from a hottie in low-risers displaying plenty of skin between her jeans and tight ribbed tank top. She turned to talk to one of the metrosexual men languishing about, and he got a squint at the elaborate tattoo on her lower back, its tendrils descended to her barely covered crack. Chambers was mightily tempted to compliment her on her tramp stamp but got his head right. His sister would kill him if he f'd this up.

Mind on my money, he admonished himself. Anyway, the honeys would be taking numbers to get with him once they pulled this off. Given this was a gathering of the cool and trendy, there was no security guard. Besides, what self-respecting stick-up artist would go for any of this stuff? It's not like a Chumash woven basket or the photos of the trolley car storage yard had street value. Chambers couldn't help but grin. Chumps.

His sister had moved to the other side of the space, faking like she was interested in a desk and chair setup said to have belonged to socialist muckraking lawyer Job Harriman. He had once come close to being the mayor of Los Angeles in the early part of the last century. That is until, some argued, his campaign was torpedoed by a conspiracy or at least a collusion of interests with the bombing of the *L.A. Times* building at its center.

A Chicano bristling with stout upper arms sidled over to her. He was definitely not rocking that in-between gender vibe. The *vato* was on the prowl for some of that artistic poon tang, Chambers reflected. The two exchanged nods and low modulated words. Maybe he should be concerned about Sally staying on point.

Chambers wheeled behind Professor Cyrus Langston who was talking to a man and woman about Talmock's head.

"It is rather amazing that the head turned up where it did." Langston sipped some of his white wine from a clear plastic cup. "But how fortunate that Wakefield Nakano brought this amazing find to our department at USC."

The older man was lanky with bowed legs, half glasses on a chain around his neck, and one of those Ahab kind of beards that had Chambers giggling when his sister had first shown him the archeologist's picture.

"How did you identify the head, professor?" the man asked. He was the studious type with a thin, gaunt face.

He explained there had been the vestiges of a headband on the mummified head and that corresponded with a known drawing of the shaman. Carbon 14 dating confirmed the time period, Langston went on.

Chambers reached around to the pouch draped on the backside of his chair. It wasn't time yet, but he needed the reassurance.

"Oh yes," Langston continued, "prior to the Emerald Shoals project that's there now, there was a building dating back to the early part of the twentieth century. I mean, even then you would have assumed the digging that went on when that structure was erected would have turned up the head or some other artifact."

"None had been found in that area before?" the woman asked in an accent Chambers couldn't place. She touched a heavy necklace around her neck as if invoking, or warding off, ancient ghosts.

Langston inclined his head. "As far as my research has yielded, there has not been any such Chumash or any other American Indian remains or items culled from that part of downtown Los Angeles. Though mind you," he added, brightening, "the former Produce Exchange Building that was there had quite a history, including murder."

"That's very interesting," the woman said, regarding her smiling companion then turning back to the academic. "What's the story, Professor Langston?"

Langston began. Seems there had been an orange grove speculator whose wife came to his office one late hot afternoon to find him involved in more than a professional way with his pretty Filipina secretary. Chambers tuned him out. His sister got into position and he casually retrieved the three oblong, hand-fashioned smoke bombs from his pouch. Using a recipe obtained online, Chambers had made the little wonders on the kitchen stove using easily obtained chemicals. He wheeled toward the restroom located along a short hallway.

The gallery owner, a handsome, running back sized woman in a flowing peasant dress with an explosion of black hair, raised her glass for attention.

"I want to thank you for coming out tonight," she began. "And I'm so pleased that Cyrus could finally be present," she indicated Langston who bowed slightly. Chambers finished counting to sixty and lit the short fuses on his smoke bombs. He prayed in case the good Lord could see fit to protect their criminal enterprise.

o o o

"IT WAS SURE GOOD SEEING you, Esther," Magrady told his daughter.

"Same here, Pop." She touched his hand, frowning slightly.

He nodded, understanding. Was this for real this time, or just a long set up to get money out of her? They sat at the dining table, a coffee cup before him and a wine glass before her. "Amazing how they grow," he added, referring to his sleeping grandkids Evelyn and Cass, short for Casina. The girls were twelve and ten, respectively. The last time they'd seen him, they'd been in their Hello Kitty PJs scared and fascinated at the mumbling drunk grandpa who fell down in their kitchen. This time they were naturally standoffish at this serious-looking old man who knew he shouldn't try too hard to gain their affection—at least on this visit.

He'd brought them an assortment of novels for young adults. That earned him a point or two right off with his wary daughter. He would have brought toys but Magrady had no idea what kind girls their age liked. Janis Bonilla had suggested the books. These gifts showed he was concerned about them broadening their minds, as Esther was a big reader, even if they didn't dig the selections. When Esther had called him back, and after they'd discussed her mother's illness, she'd asked him to come out for dinner tonight, Saturday. It wasn't lost on Magrady that it was a way for her to size up her pops without having to worry about him taking the girls to a movie or amusement park. She was willing to see him, but she didn't trust him.

Well, Magrady fondly assessed, he and Claudelia had raised their daughter right to be no one's fool, especially when a family member was involved. A comfortable silence ebbed between them. He eventually asked, "Say, you mind if I look through some of those boxes I left you before I get going?"

"You could spend the night, you know. We have the spare room."

"For sure next time."

She zeroed him with a look. "This big case of yours you have to solve."

He spread his arms.

"Come on." Unnecessarily she led the way through her townhouse in the now aging, but comfortable, subdivision. Newer, shinier ones had bloomed around her. It had been some time, but he did know the way as the attached garage was accessible through a side door off the kitchen.

At twenty-three, Esther had married one of those enterprising brothers who'd attended Howard, did the stomp pledge for Alpha Phi Alpha, and attended grad school at Stanford. Rod Delaney started and sold off various successful businesses from a limo service specializing in ferrying pro athletes to several chain sandwich shops placed strategically in two malls out here in

Diamond Bar and other parts of San Bernardino. Early on he'd made a deal with a developer of those malls before the entity was swallowed by SubbaKhan, closing some of his stores in the process. But by then his hard-charging son-in-law had invested in new enterprises.

Though he was conscious of his diet and worked out on his stationary bike, Delaney's total workaholic drive silently ate at his insides, and four years ago he'd had a fatal heart attack at thirty-nine. Esther Delaney Magrady, (the name's rhythmic cadence a song her children liked to sing,) sold off most of the investments. Thereafter she made studied and conservative stock market investments toward the girls' college fund while maintaining her career as a clothes buyer for the Tilson department store chain. She'd been well poised to ride out the economic downturn when it hit.

"Need any help?" she asked from the top step as her father sifted through the stacked, and mostly unmarked, cardboard boxes. Now they were all on one side of the two-car space, once having been pushed to the rear. But Esther only needed the sole family van these days.

"I'm okay, Chongo."

He used to call her that goofy name when she was a kid. It used to make her wince as a teen when he did it in front of her friends and he'd been weaned off doing it by enough "Daddy, please" pleadings. Now it made her nostalgic. She left him to his digging.

He'd opened a rectangular box that contained the tool belt he wore as a cable installer, along with wires, alligator clips, voltage regulator and so on that he'd used back then as well as when he was doing security systems installations. He'd also worked as a beer truck driver and tire and tune up mechanic at Pep Boys. Fingering an old work shirt with his nametag sewn on it, Magrady revisited the jobs he'd had, most of them punching the man's clock.

But there was a period in the late '80s with a couple of buddies from the service when he'd been his own boss. Together they'd started a magazine and paperback distribution business. The partners had put their money together and bought a two and a half-ton cargo truck used in 'Nam. They rebuilt the engine and swapped out the differential. One of the buddies knew a local writer who churned out crime potboilers for a mass-market division operated by a skin mag king. Because the publisher didn't like the percentage cut he was getting from his mainstream distributor, he gave the virgin operation a shot. And given Magrady had contacts with liquor stores in South Central, Watts, and Compton due to his beer delivery days, this opened up new territory for the girlie mags and paperbacks.

Things were going so good at one point the partnership was able to purchase two newer vans. But it turned out the nudie magnate managed cash flow situations via a three-hundred-acre pot farm outside of Arcata near the Oregon border. His bust led to the dissolution of his company and their lucrative business. Magrady didn't exactly rebound from that setback. Rather, given he'd been introduced to the wonders of powdered cocaine at a few Topanga Canyon parties the paperback writer had invited them to, he figured to seek answers in an enlightened state. How shocking the blow didn't make him wiser, only more broke and more pitiful to his wife and kids.

There in a small box containing amongst other items his Distinguished Service medal and Combat Infantryman's badge, he found his disassembled army-issued .45 wrapped in a square of cotton over an oil cloth. He rewrapped the handgun, and along with some other personal flotsam, put everything in a paper shopping bag he'd taken from the kitchen. He wanted to take this small clay bear his son had made for him in first grade. But it wasn't like he was going to have an office anytime soon where he could use it for a paperweight as he did back in the distribution days. Certainly moving about as he always had to do, it would get broken. Carefully, he packed the bear away again.

"All set," he said to Esther as he re-entered the living room carrying his grocery bag like it was an oversized lunch. She was reclining on the couch, her head back with a contented look on her face. The pre-paid cell phone he'd bought vibrated in his pocket. That had to be the call from Sid Ramos. The robbery must have gone down. Outside was a rented car Angie Baine had obtained for him. That was one solid chick.

"Heard your brother is in New York City. Know anything about that?"

"A little."

"Yes?"

She worried her lower lip. "This is all kind of vague, okay, Pop? But I got the impression it was some kind of Madoff jive."

Early on, his son had demonstrated a facility for math. He'd gone on to be in several mathematic decathlons in school. Funny how both his kids had a facility for numbers—definitely from their mother. "Wonderful, stock swindles or some such?"

She gave him a feeble look.

"Anything you can find out, you know."

"Yeah," she let the rest go unsaid. She and her brother had lost touch with each other as well.

"If nothing else, I want to tell him about Mom."

"I'll see what I can do," she said.

"Good."

He kissed her on the forehead as she gave his arm a squeeze. They remained embraced for several moments and when each let go, they smiled at each other, their eyes teary. He got going, promising to call her next week. In the car, Magrady hoped he wouldn't screw it up this time. He had learned, more than once, there was no blueprint for life, that relationships required attention and constant adjustments, not retreat. Driving on the freeway, he phoned El Cid.

"You should have seen it, man," his fellow vet said, happily. "It was like one of those caper flicks. I'm hunkered down outside like we planned. These artsy and pinhead types are gabbing inside and genuflecting over this or that in the exhibit. Though let me tell you there were some fine *heinas* up in there, Em. Damn.

"So anyway, the dragon puffs and smoke fills the gallery. I hear a woman's voice, probably Floyd's sister, yelling fire. Naturally these candy-ass civilians hurry their rarified selves to the sidewalk. Then from this side street as a fire truck approaches, I spot a Camry light out."

"How'd you know it was them?"

"First off, if it was you that just ran out, would you book? No. You'd hang around and see the show."

"Good point."

"Uh-huh. Plus I'm using night binocs and couldn't miss Floyd's big head in the car."

They both laughed.

"They came back to an apartment near Midway Hospital." He gave him the location on Curson in Mid-City Los Angeles.

"I'm on my way," Magrady said.

"Hold on," El Cid said, "they're coming back out."

"Shit."

"Get to steppin', brother . . . "

VIII

"YOU SURE YOU DON'T WANT me to take the stroll with you?" El Cid asked Magrady. Cold air condensed around his mouth as he spoke.

The vets stood inside a tunnel leading to the stands and field of SubbaKhan's Bixby Stadium in Long Beach, past two in the morning. There had been a night crew prepping the grounds but they'd left about an hour ago. Cold air visibly billowed from their mouths as the two talked in low voices in the tunnel. Outside, a fog was coming in off the ocean, enveloping the open-air structure in heavy layers.

Magrady stared beyond the end of the passageway. "I can't lay that on you, home."

"You and me ain't no virgins," his friend answered. "We've both been guests in the Greybar Hotel."

"I'll be all right. Nakano came alone. And you reconned the perimeter, so what's to worry?"

"I'm older than you, Em, that's the worry. I damn sure might have missed something. Eyes and senses are going quick. And this situation feels . . . ghoulish. What's he want that god-damn head for? And why the fuck meet here?"

Magrady cinched his coat tighter. "I'll ask him, big dog." He clapped him on the arm. "Go on, get some breakfast." He offered a folded twenty.

El Cid ignored the gesture and clamping his teeth, grunted,

"Tell you what, I'll hang here. I hear commotion, the cops come rolling up on silent, something like that, I'll signal you."

He didn't want to get his friend in trouble but if he argued with him to leave, he'd be insulted. El Cid needed purpose just as Magrady did. "Cool."

When the former Lurp had called Magrady on his way back from Diamond Bar and his reunion with his daughter, Chambers and his sister were on the move from what both assumed was her apartment in Mid-City.

"Can you delay them?" Magrady had asked El Cid over the cell phone.

"What, like ram their car?"

"That's a bit more drastic than I had in mind. How about letting the air out of one of their tires?"

"But they're already outside."

Magrady shot back, "You can't create a diversion? You're deep in country, soldier, improvise."

"Fuck." He hung up, got out of his car, and, ducking behind some shrubbery, let out a mighty scream. He wasn't much of a movie fan, but he'd had an uncle who'd come to L.A. from El Paso in '49. His Uncle Rafael had designs on being an actor, but the one casting director he did manage to get in to see had groused, "We already have a Mexican on our roster." The racist notion being that one Mexican was like any other when it came to parts in the realm of make believe. Whites had individuality, everybody else was just a type.

But Uncle Rafael did wrangle a job as the aging Bela Lugosi's driver, picking him up at his modest home in the Leimert Park section and taking him around to auditions for Grade C films, and sometimes having to score the old man's dope. So that's why El Cid had bothered to rent the biopic about Ed Wood. He was able to call up the scene with Martin Landau as the strung-out Lugosi screaming like a man afire as he's attacked by a rubber octopus. The torment expressed in his character's threadbare existence inhabited the yell. It was a cry that resonated with El Cid in an inarticulate but down-in-his-bones way. All that shit he still carried with him from the nightmare of 'Nam was in his scream in the bushes.

This got doors opened and heads at windows. The Camry Chambers had come in was down the block, as El Cid had parked near them. As everyone was in stop frame trying to figure out who was getting murdered, he was able to creep along, down low behind the cars at the curb on the street side. He got to their car. Using the point of one of his keys, he pressed it into the end of the valve stem and depressed the inner mechanism to deflate the tire. He was going to do a second one but figured they would know they were being purposely delayed.

By the time Floyd Chambers and his sister changed the tire, neither being particularly mechanically inclined, Magrady was halfway back to town and transferred to yet another freeway. Thereafter the siblings were heading to the stadium trailed by El Cid. When the brother and sister got to the stadium, they had to wait more than a half-hour in their car. Eventually a darkly gleaming Mercedes pulled up and the two vets spied Nakano getting out and letting Chambers and his sister inside a side entrance, which locked back into place.

"No time for half-stepping," Magrady mumbled.

"Damn right," El Cid agreed.

Magrady trotted down the remaining length of the tunnel. There would be no cheers from a crowd or replay on the Jumbotron. He paused to light a ball of bunched up newspapers as he approached the end of the tunnel. He and El Cid assumed the other three were up in Nakano's private box concluding their business. Given how El Cid dressed and having gotten a hold of a rake, he'd blended in with the mostly Latino grounds crew walking in and out of the then open outer security gates. El Cid had hunkered inside when the workers had departed and let Magrady in via a thick metal service door, the kind with a crash bar on the inside and a keyed lock, no handle, on the outside.

Magrady tossed the ball out onto the grass and as it flared up he stepped close to his personal bonfire, knowing he could be seen in the gloomy arena. He cupped his hands to the side of his mouth and yelled, "Hey, you rapscallions, where's my cut?"

For several moments the only sound was the crackling of his quickly diminishing fireball. Then a light high up came on, and over the PA Wakefield Nakano's voice echoed through the pall. "Why don't you come on up, Mr. Magrady?"

"Don't mind if I do," he said. He ascended the steps toward the luxury boxes and arrived at a door partially left open for him. Stepping through, Sally Chambers waited just inside. She leveled an efficient-looking .22 Beretta on his belly.

"Don't think I don't know how to use this, chump. This way," she jerked her head indicating a hallway behind her.

Magrady did as ordered. She clicked the door back into place and even if El Cid in spirit had his back, there was no way he was getting in. Magrady was on his own. So be it. Gun at his back, he pushed open an ajar door to the executive boxes. They passed through a suite Magrady assumed must belong to an exec, as it was clearly a working office. On a wall among framed awards and certificates, was a picture of a handsome woman in her forties and what he took to be her grown daughter. They wore matching stylish glasses. He stared at it as light spilled into the room from an open door at the far end.

"Losing your nerve there, Sergeant Saunders?" Sally Chambers taunted. She poked him in the back to get going. They went through the open door and through another doorway.

"Pretty swank, Floyd. You've done well for yourself." Magrady took in the luxury suite with its built-in marble wet bar, widescreen plasma TV, plush chairs, matching couches and Agra throw rugs. The disabled man had a drink in his hand and a burning cigar in the other.

"Live like Snoop," he answered, saluting him with the drink. He took a long puff and let out a stream.

Magrady tried not to interpret the smoke as his future blowing away. He came further into the suite. "As you've always wanted." Talmock's head was again in a clear case and rested on a desk where Wakefield Nakano, dressed in slacks and knit shirt, leaned against it with arms folded.

"We need to do something about him," Sally Chambers said, moving away from him but still keeping her piece steady on the uninvited guest.

"Like you did Savoirfaire?" Magrady drilled her with a look. She snickered. "We had nothing to do with that."

Nakano unfolded his arms and said, "I'm sure you're a rational man, Mr. Magrady."

"I like to think I am."

The sister looked from Nakano to her brother. "What? Pay him off?"

Nakano massaged his hands together though it was pleasantly warm in the suite. "It's the rational thing to do."

"But he knows about us," she protested.

"He's gonna be cool," her brother said. He'd placed the drink on an end table and worked the cigar between two fingers and thumb. "What it gonna take, Em? Five, ten thousand, sound good?"

"Shit yeah," Magrady enthused.

With the seven hundred and some odd dollars he got a month from the VA and what he made under the table doing odd jobs like being a bouncer at a backyard *Quinceañera* keeping drunks from throwing up on the birthday girl's pretty dress or fixing the brakes on an Urban Advocacy organizer's car, any amount with a comma in it sounded about right.

"But," he added, "it's not you two stealing the head on orders from Nakano here that's the issue, is it?"

"How's that?" Sally Chambers grinned sideways.

"Somebody killed Savoirfaire and made me the goat for it. Is that why you came to me, Floyd? Played on our friendship to put me against him so that when you took him out, the spotlight was on me while y'all planned your little caper?"

"It wasn't like that, Em. You know me better than that."

"Savoirfaire got wind of you and this damn head." The mummified shaman regarded Magrady impassively. "Bet you were high, huh, Floyd. I know how you like to get your buzz on."

Chambers looked contrite.

"No, it was Boo Boo," Magrady corrected, remembering the thug's stoplight eyes when he first encountered him in the Hornet's Hive bar. "You two were sparkin' up and you got to braggin', didn't you, Floyd? You caught yourself when you were with me and Janis, but you let it slip with your boy."

"You tellin' it." Floyd Chambers placed the cigar in an ashtray and then interlaced his fingers on his lap.

"So that puts the Gold Dust Twins on your ass and why you went gopher."

Chambers snorted and his sister said irritably, "See?" Sally Chambers shook the gun at Magrady. "He's going to be a problem."

"And you know how to deal with problems, don't you, Sally?"

"You're talking nonsense." She moved closer to Nakano who smiled thinly at her.

"Yeah, well, somebody caved in homeboy's noggin." As Magrady talked, he shifted his position, angling himself between the two at the desk and Chambers in his wheelchair.

Magrady hooked a thumb at his friend, "I still don't see Floyd being that devious, but you are." He pointed at the sister. "You'd already chilled your old man for tippin' out on you on the down low. I suppose that insulted your sense of womanhood."

She bared teeth at him.

Magrady continued. "Nakano had already cooked this up. Though why he would come to the both of you to steal the head . . . oh," he paused. "You were bangin' the boss."

Sally Chambers jerked the gun upward at Magrady but Nakano gently placed a hand on her arm. The SubbaKhan executive said tersely, "What will it take to satisfy you, Mr. Magrady?"

"Twenty, no twenty-five thousand for all the bullshit y'all put me through."

"Everybody's got their hand out," Sally Chambers sneered.

"So fill it," he said.

"And if we don't?"

"You gonna do me like you did Savoirfaire, Sally?"

Her brother gripped his wheels, tightly. "Get off that, Em."

Magrady continued. "She did him, didn't she? She took care of that clown. I know like a fat man loves Ding Dongs, Savoirfaire had a thing for your baby sis, huh? He'd invite her over to his crib to talk things over, licking his lips like the puffed up fool he was."

Nakano and Sally Chambers exchanged indecipherable looks.

The sister charged forward, the gun on Magrady. "Stop talking like I'm not here, asshole."

He put up his hands and took a few steps away from her. "Okay, all right, my bad, Annie Oakley. Don't shoot."

Nakano began, "Look, let's reason this out."

Magrady pretended to stumble walking backward, falling to the floor sideways on his hip. As he did he stuck a hand in his jacket pocket and blew out a hole with his service automatic. If he was a better shot, he would have been clever and took out the light switch like he'd seen in this '50s crime movie with Charles McGraw. But he knew his limitations and instead aimed above Sally Chambers' head, getting her to duck. He scrambled on his stomach and knees and came up in a crouch behind Floyd Chambers' chair.

"Please, please, this isn't necessary," Nakano pleaded. "Sally, honey, we can resolve this."

"How, Wake," she yelled. "Money?"

"Yes," he said testily. "Isn't that always the answer for what ails us?"

"But he knows, Wake," she insisted.

"Shut up, Sally," her brother said. He looked over his shoulder. "We can work this out, right, Em?" Sweat dripped off his strained face.

"Tell her to drop the heater," Magrady demanded.

"Fuck that," she snorted. "Get out from behind my brother."

Magrady had a tight grip on Floyd Chambers' upper shoulder, his gun peaking from around the seated man. "What about that dough, Wakefield?"

"Yes, come on, let's all get a grip." He stood away from the desk, his hands out like a man signaling to halt an oncoming vehicle. "This is bigger than just matters of greed."

"Oh, I'm greedy now," Sally Chambers blurted. "Sorry I don't have the wonderful magic grand vision you have . . . hon. Guess you can take the girl out of the ghetto and all that."

"Look, baby, this is so much more than that. You know what this means to me."

"And what about me?" she demanded.

"Y'all got issues." Magrady shot upright and raising his foot, propelled Floyd Chambers into his sister. She fired her gun at him but the Vietnam vet went flat and shot her in the thick of her thigh. She howled and bent over to grab her leg as her brother took the gun from her hand.

"That's enough, Sal."

Nakano had the head cradled like a football under his arm and was already through another doorway. Magrady chased after him, briefly taking in brother and sister holding on to each other as he ran after the escaping man and the head of the lost Aztec, Talmock.

Wakefield Nakano was already through a metal door at the end of the hallway, opposite from where from where Magrady had entered. He ran after the CEO, sorry that he didn't work out more and lamenting his advancing years. But damn that. Old ass notwithstanding, he was going to catch this clown and shake some answers out of him.

Magrady leaned his shoulder to the door and popped the crash bar. He stepped into a dimly lit narrow stairwell where he could hear Nakano's footsteps descending. Having the advantage of empty hands, Magrady grabbed the railing on either side of the stairs and was able to jump over several steps at a time by hoisting himself aloft and sliding down. Still, when he reached the bottom, Nakano had made it out the exit.

Close on him, Magrady found himself back outside in the cold and fog. Security lights snapped on as his body triggered their sensors but little of their illumination pierced the soup. Momentarily disoriented, he crept forward, straining to hear and locate himself. He was glad there weren't alarms whooping or security guards around to interfere. Nakano must have seen to that. For this was his mission to complete. Magrady didn't give a shit about headlines or glory or getting his face on the nightly news. It just felt so goddamn good he'd stuck with this from start to finish—even if that meant him winding up face down or doing a jolt in the joint. He'd seen it through and he couldn't say that about much else in several years.

Stalking forward in the muck, his shoes sounded dully on the asphalt. Feeling to his left his hand came upon the moist metal skin of the arena. Logic told him they must have come out somewhere near Nakano's Mercedes. Or at least that's where he'd have to be heading. Magrady concentrated to call up the layout of the stadium's perimeter in his head. He debated yelling for El Cid. That's when something disturbed the space in front of him causing him to instinctively rear back.

Magrady swung his fist but only went through air, the form having evaporated. Whatever Nakano had swung at him he was pretty sure it wasn't the plastic case with Talmock's head in it. He wouldn't mess up his prize. He also had the impression the exec hadn't done all this just to have the artifact for some sort of secret collection. But this wasn't the time to be distracted. He turned to his right, expecting Nakano to come at him on the flank. That's what he'd do. The form reappeared before him.

Magrady lashed out with his foot chest high and earned a grunt from his adversary. But he retreated again into the pall. How the fuck was this chump pinpointing him, Magrady wondered. Was that goddamn head responsible? Maybe it really did have magic properties and was talking to him. Shit.

Magrady smiled grimly at that notion as he crouched and holding his arms out, swept the area in front of him as he darted this way and that. He collided with Nakano who whapped the vet on his forearm with an object.

"Fuck," he hollered. Nakano had hit him with a polo mallet. Figures. He must have had it in his car. Gritting his teeth from the pain, Magrady ducked below away the mallet aimed at his head, having heard it whistle toward him. Nakano could have driven away but decided to stay and fight it out. He wanted to punish him for interfering. Where was the peace and calmness in that?

The blunt mallet arched out of the fog again and banged Magrady on his bicep as he turned his body trying unsuccessfully to avoid the blow. Ignoring the throbbing in his arm, he lunged and almost got his arms around the executive. But the other man was elusive and jammed a knee into the underside of Magrady's jaw. Down on all fours, he rolled and the mallet struck him on the back of his shoulder blades.

"Defiler," Nakano said as Magrady latched on to his ankle and yanked, causing the younger man to stumble backward but not go over.

Magrady got to his feet. Each circled the other, no more than five feet apart. Plenty of room for that polo-lovin' prick to hit him again he assessed unemotionally. "The fuck you talking about, Nakano? What's this ugly-ass mummy head mean to you?"

"Don't pretend with me, Magrady. I see what this is. That's why you haven't used your gun. I might have hidden the head and if I'm dead, you might not find it in time."

"Glad you've seen through me." He hesitated threatening to shoot a man with Nakano's considerable resources. But whatever it was about Talmock's head, it had him in thrall. He held the plastic mallet tight in his hand at an angle from his body, ready to strike. "Why'd you want the head back so badly, man?"

"The same reason you want it. You know its promise. Why else would somebody like you keep at this? Why you mustn't stop me," Nakano asserted.

"Wakefield," Sally Chambers yelled through the fog.

Magrady couldn't pinpoint her. "I've got people here too, Nakano," he told the other man, implying the authorities were on their way. Of course the last damn thing either he or El Cid would do was call the law. But Floyd's sister might have talked her big bro into giving her back her piece and that made him nervous.

Suddenly Nakano was in front of him and was swinging the mallet at his rib cage. Magrady tucked in his arm and took the hit on his elbow, earning an audible crack of bone. But he put what he had into a punch with his left hand, and tagged the SubbaKhan chief flush on the face. His right arm was tingling with numbness but Magrady pressed on. He threw his body into Nakano's, knocking him over. Standing over him, he reached across and pulled his gun free from his jacket pocket.

"Let go of the mallet or I let one loose in your kneecap."

Nakano stared up at him with disgust but did as ordered.

Behind him Magrady sensed a presence and from the look on Nakano's face, he could tell it wasn't Sally Chambers. He said, "Glad you made it, El. Better keep sharp, there's a pissed off sister limping around with a bullet I put in her and a gat she knows how to use. Floyd's here too."

"On it," he said and allowed the fog to envelope him as he faded away to look for the sister.

"What happened between the time Talmock's head was dug up and you turning it over to the university and now?" Magrady asked Nakano who stood up. "Why all this to get it back? And what promise are you talking about?"

The executive smiled like a man with the winning hand. "So you really don't know."

Magrady resisted the impulse to slap him silly with the barrel of the gun. "That all you got to say?"

Nakano chuckled mirthlessly, "It would seem." He adopted a shrewd look. "I should probably call my lawyer."

"Fuck that," Magrady said and advanced, giving in to impulse. "You don't get to hide behind your $600-an-hour shysters, Nakano. I'm going to get the goddamn truth out of you." Magrady jabbed the gun in Nakano's stomach like Boo Boo had done him.

"Told you play time was over," Magrady growled at Nakano's surprised face.

Before the assault escalated, Floyd Chambers rushed out of the fog in his wheelchair and collided with Magrady. He tumbled into Chambers' lap and the wheelchair fell over on its side. Nakano ran away as Chambers used his overdeveloped arms to grapple with his the vet.

"Come on, Floyd, cut this shit out."

"Can't let you ef up my payday, man."

Magrady felt bad but clubbed him on the top of his head with the butt of the .45, dazing him and allowing the vet to scramble loose. The Mercedes' engine turned over and its headlights reflected on the ever-present grey, coming in their direction. Magrady turned and dragged Chambers out of the way as the car careened through the thick mist, the passenger side missing them by inches. Magrady's back to the wall, the car scraped against the side of the stadium ahead of them. Nakano looked back but Magrady had raised his gun. Nakano roared away. Magrady was glad. He knew damn well Nakano's lawyers would have put him away for the rest of his sorry-ass natural life if he'd have put a slug in the CEO.

El Cid appeared before him, smiling.

IX

LAPD CAPTAIN LOREN STOVER shook a finger at Magrady. "I don't believe a goddamn thing you have to say."

"Like I give a fuck."

"Gentlemen," attorney Gordon Walters said in a soothing tone, "let's try to keep the rancor at a minimum, shall we?"

Hands on his hips, Stover stalked around the interrogation room inside the Nickel Squad's headquarters in the former Greyhound Bus station. "You don't have any evidence supporting this bullshit claim of yours that Sally Chambers did in said unfortunate."

Sitting side by side at a metal table with a handcuff rail, Walters put a hand on Magrady's arm to stop him from reacting and spoke. "Investigating this is not our job, Captain. The fact remains that there are witnesses placing Chambers and his sister at the gallery, coupled with my client's assertion that they stole the mummified head and delivered same to the now missing Wakefield Nakano."

"Who Dolemite here might have knocked off like he did Savoirfaire," Stover added.

"As you would say, there is no evidence supporting that claim," Walters countered. "There is evidence, as Mr. Magrady has said, Nakano came at him and Floyd Chambers with his vehicle. I have the results of the paint scrapings taken from Bixby Stadium and they match the factory batch of paint used on the model of the Mercedes registered to Mr. Nakano."

"That could have been from anything. He backed up and accidentally hit the side of the building."

"Find him and ask him, Captain." Walters looked at Magrady who stared at Stover. "But so far the district attorney has not charged my client nor do I believe in light of these new facts that he has unearthed, will he do so."

"Isn't that lovely?" Stover mumbled, glaring at an ochre-colored wall.

"We're done for now, Captain." Walters and Magrady rose.

At the door Magrady said, "Hey, Stover."

"What, numbnuts?"

Genially he asked, "You ever suck a dick sweeter than mine?"

It took Walters and two uniforms to separate Magrady and Stover.

o o o

MAGRADY BORROWED THE MONEY for the camping fees from his lawyer Gordon Walters and used a pup tent and some camping equipment Red Spencer lent him. The crash site where the experimental Serpent's Wing had gone down was deemed off-limits but it wasn't much of an effort to hike into that area. The military guards had been reassigned and any evidence of any scrap of equipment had been dutifully removed.

He'd been camping out for several days, getting in some fishing and re-reading two books by a writer named Leon Ray Livingston, *From Coast to Coast* and the *Trail of the Tramp*. As a young man, traveling with the moniker A-No. 1, Livingston was the self-described King of the Hobos, inspiring Jack London as well as being the basis for a character in a movie made in the '70s. After his time riding the rails had passed, Livingston, who kept journals of the road, published and lectured about his colorful life. Reportedly he would give a disillusioned youngster taking up the life of a 'bo, money to get home and pursue some other calling.

Magrady circled the crash site once again on the fourth day late in the afternoon. That night when Nakano nearly ran he and Floyd Chambers down, and the car had stopped for a few beats, Magrady had glimpsed a map labeled of the Cleveland National Forest displayed on the Mercedes' dash navigation system. His guess was Nakano in his present state attached significance to where the plane went down as some sort of nexus of the hoodoo that had a grip on him. The name of the craft, the Serpent's Wing, could be interpreted as a symbol meaning the feathered serpent, Quetzalcoatl, the Aztec deity.

Emerging from heavy foliage on a rise, he spotted Nakano lying atop a rock outcropping several yards below him. He wasn't dressed in traditional Chumash or Aztec garb as he'd imagined. Not that Magrady knew what such clothing would look like given that, like most Americans, his reference points were western movies or those reruns of the *Tales of Wells Fargo* TV show with Dale Robertson he liked as a kid. Nakano was in a wet suit, Talmock's head in netting strapped to a belt around his waist. There was a sheathed knife attached to the belt as well.

Magrady hadn't chanced sneaking his pistol into the park considering he didn't have a license for it. But he had brought his own knife, a serrated blade he'd tucked next to his ankle, anchored in the heavy soled shoe he wore. Nakano spied on men and women splashing and swimming in a stream down below him at the bottom of the basin. Magrady wasn't sure what was going through the mix-master brain of the VP's head, but it had occurred to him Nakano had come out here maybe on the lookout for a human sacrifice or two for his old pard, Talmock. That was the reason for the wet suit, for blood splash.

Magrady bounced a small rock near Nakano, missing his head which he'd aimed at. The other man turned from where he lay splayed on the rock. Blinking uncomprehendingly at first, he then registered his stalker. "You," he sneered and skittered backward off the rock like a lizard.

In motion as well, the older man could hear Nakano running through the brush and he jogged in a diagonal direction as he descended the hill. He came into an opening in time to see Nakano sprinting toward a dirt bike he'd obviously pushed to this location so as to be silent.

"Aw, shit," Magrady huffed and leaped, coming down hard on the other man. They tumbled over and over, Magrady's shoulder having partially hit the ground causing him to grit his teeth, pain starring behind his eyes.

"Cut it out, you crazy fuck," Magrady blared as the two men tussled. Nakano smacked him along the jaw with his elbow and, crab-like, scrambled clear of his attacker. He got to his feet, having dislodged his knife. Magrady scooted backward, kicking up gravel as curious squirrels watched the two from the tree limbs. He rolled and grabbed his blade free as well. Breathing hard he also got to his feet.

"Why don't you calm the fuck down, and let's have a sit-down, Nakano." Magrady was going to defend himself, but off his nut or not, he was worried what kind of heat would befall him should he have to skewer the SubbaKhan exec.

"You don't understand. I'm chosen." Nakano's sweating face was painted with designs Magrady took as mystic Aztec symbols. Some were etched in his skin.

"Don't worry, with your money, they'll choose a quiet room with nice wallpaper attended by nurses with cleavage to make Beyoncé jealous."

"You make fun while the cosmos teeters, Magrady." He swept forward, making cutting motions with the knife. Magrady blocked the first thrust with his knife, but the second attack sliced into his forearm muscle and Magrady lashed out with his foot, catching Nakano in the side. If he let up Nakano would have him. He grabbed onto the wrist of the man's knife hand to immobilize the threat and simultaneously he stabbed Nakano in the upper chest, toward the shoulder area. Not enough, he hoped, to kill, just to incapacitate.

Nakano whooshed air and staggered back, still holding his knife.

"Drop it," Magrady ordered. "I can stop the bleeding."

Nakano threw the knife underhanded at Magrady who dove aside, the damn thing nicking his butt cheek. The other man ran off.

Magrady landed on his knee and wasn't capable of going after the addled exec. He sat, his legs drawn up, getting his energy back. Eventually he rose, dusting the dirt off the back of his pants.

"Bastard," he mumbled, limping off.

Magrady was by no stretch some kind of outdoorsman who could track a quarry though the woods like some Louis

L'Amour character. But asking around after he'd tidied himself up produced results. Particularly this retired couple listening to swing music sitting outside their Winnebago.

"Yes, sir," the balding man said, pointing in a northerly direction. "We did see your friend, this Asian fella, head that'a way. He seemed to be favoring his shoulder."

"That is so," the woman affirmed. "Had a wetsuit all balled up under his arm. Like you see surfers use, but there's no place to surf around here." She looked up at Magrady for an explanation but he only smiled crookedly. Her hair was dyed a flame sunset orange.

"He had this lost look to him," the woman added, returning her attention to what she'd been doing. She was using what looked like a dentist's probe on a small slab of ivory, etching an image of bears sailing a schooner.

"Thank you kindly," he said, moving off.

"Our pleasure," the man said. He resumed reading his lesbian romance novel. On the cover were two bronzed women, one in a bikini, the other in a business suit, hefting a gun.

It didn't take Magrady long to find Wakefield Nakano's campsite. He was set up near a smooth rock face splotched with grey-green moss. He seemed to have bandaged his wound and was staring at Talmock's head, perched incongruously on the seat of a folding canvas chair. Magrady entered the clearing.

"Look, Nakano, I'm not going to let you run around here playing slasher. You need help. Time to di di mau," using the expression from his 'Nam days meaning to get going in a hurry.

He looked quizzically at Magrady, tilting his head, but didn't reply.

Magrady stepped closer. "Let me," but before he could finish, Nakano rushed him, snarling like a cornered wolf. He bowled Magrady over, clawing and biting at him, consumed in a feral state.

As the birds chirped in the bucolic setting, Nakano decided to replay the Tyson-Holyfield rematch and he chomped down on Magrady's ear. He started gnawing on it.

"Goddammit," Magrady hollered, finally and desperately getting the flashlight loose he'd brought along in his back pocket. He clubbed the top of the younger man's head, eliciting blood and stillness.

"This is getting to be a bad habit," he groused, referring to how he'd also just thumped Floyd Chambers the same way.

Magrady then staunched his new wound and using his disposable cell phone, made a call into the ranger's station—having logged the number before his excursion. He wasn't too worried about his blood or other types of trace evidence tying him to the attack. They'd wash out the wounded man's mouth and by the time it was determined Nakano hadn't fallen as Magrady said over the phone, all sorts of contamination of the evidence would have occurred. Nakano might well implicate him but he figured Gordon Walters could mount plausible deniability against a man on his way to the mental ward—even a well-to-do one.

He slipped away in the oncoming gloom, carrying Talmock's head in a plastic bag he'd found in Nakano's tent.

X

"THANKS, JANIS." MAGRADY SAID to his friend over his recently acquired cell phone. "I keep owing you. And I don't mean just money."

"Just find your son, big dog. I'm'a hold it down on my end. The Emerald Shoals opening is tonight and I plan to slap the shit out of that turncoat ho Amy on local TV."

"Take it easy, champ." When Magrady had gone to Bixby Stadium on the hunt for Talmock's head, he'd spotted a photograph of Amy Rogers with an older version of herself, her mother, also in the outer suite Sally Chambers had marched him through. He'd seen this Amy at the Urban Advocacy offices and an event or two as the young woman was supposed to be an intern with the organization. But it turned out she was doing opposition spying for SubbaKhan. Rogers' mother was the stadium's manager.

"Yeah, yeah," Bonilla said. "We've worked out a more subtle plan of disinformation to feed Amy's treacherous ass. Get SubbaKhan's panties all twisted up."

"Right on. See you when I'm back."

"Bet."

Magrady severed the call and stepped from the vestibule of Diamond Desmond's check cashing and jerk chicken emporium onto Flatbush Avenue. Bonilla had wired him four hundred and fifty dollars minus the transfer fee. The search for his son Luke had begun with the initial lead provided by Angie Baine's son Chad Talbot. Subsequently, his daughter Esther had talked to a financial planner friend living in Brooklyn who was able to provide information as well.

This took him to places like Willets Point and Red Hook, until he'd tapped out the funds he'd brought with him to New York. But running down one last lead in a used bookstore in Tribeca, where a pleasant chat with an ex-girlfriend of his son had provided some fresh names—some of whom were unpleasant folks she'd warned him not to engage.

Magrady was on the prowl for one of these unpleasants who went by the colorful sobriquet of Kang Fu.

On an earlier call, Bonilla had told him about a piece that'd run on the local news. Wakefield Nakano was said to have voluntarily stepped down from his post at SubbaKhan and was rumored to be recuperating at an undisclosed location, possibly out of the country. The article stated that in college Nakano had been a cultural anthropology undergrad and various rare books on early California history, the Aztecs and their rituals, and other such readings were found in his home.

Bonilla added an interesting bit to that. From a friend of a friend she heard that a contractor for SubbaKhan, who was part American Indian, said that as he and Nakano were heading to a meeting once, the exec had asked him about his beliefs. That did he think the Great Serpent could come forth again as it had in the past. This about a month before the head was stolen.

"What'd he say to that?" Magrady had asked her.

"What can you say when the guy who is the boss of your boss says something crazy? He told him he'd sure check into that the next time he went to the sweat lodge."

They'd laughed over that. Now Magrady was down in the subway, getting information from the lady in the booth as to the right train to take to his destination. Several minutes later he was riding along, working out his sketchy plan. He was not foolish enough to believe he could run up on this Kang Fu, particularly on his home court. But it seemed he might have a way to bait him into more neutral ground, psychologically speaking.

He exited from the F train and subway, and walked a couple of blocks to the Bowery. This was the Lower East Side. What Magrady knew about it was from old lore where movie tough guys like James Cagney and John Garfield hailed, as well as a dude named Jacob Kurtzberg. Becoming storyteller Jack Kirby, he plotted and drew a lot of the exciting comic books like *Fantastic Four* and *Thor* Magrady loved to read when he was a kid.

Now this area was called the LES by the trendies as it was being transformed into high end lofts and sparkling hotels where the peasants were only allowed to gaze at the exteriors. He meandered about. At Houston and Ludlow, he was pleased to see that Katz's Delicatessen was still there though it in the shadow of a condo on the southeast corner. He warmly recalled back in the mid-'70s spending a month in this town with a free spirited ex-army nurse named LaRose. They hung at places like CBGB's, and she going down on him in her heels in a back room of a bar called The Benjamin, named for the title character in the *Death Wish* book and films. He walked back west toward where CBGB's once was on Bowery. Now the space was occupied by some sort of designer shoe store for women.

On Great Jones Street among too-cool art galleries, he located the new-age type restaurant and bookstore called Zambroso. The place was owned by Kang Fu. Magrady entered and pretended to browse. The ex-girlfriend had shown him a cell phone picture of the supposed Kang Fu taken at a book launch at this store. The shot was of a lanky youngish man, smoothly bald, who looked like he was either a light-skinned black man, Middle Eastern or East Indian. Magrady didn't expect to simply stumble into him here. He'd been informed by the ex that Kang Fu had other concerns, and wasn't much in the store in the afternoon hours—if at all.

There was a pretty young woman in a bright print dress behind the counter. Puerto Rican and something else he estimated. She finished talking to a customer who'd bought a picture book about bridges and bats. He came over.

"Hello," Magrady said, reaching for the digital print he'd brought with him.

"And you," she answered, a pert smile illuminating her face. Her eyes briefly went to his bandaged ear then back to his face.

"Let Kang Fu know I have Talmock's head." Magrady placed the print before her on the counter. "I understand he appreciates one-of-a-kind items."

She picked it up, studying the shot. "He'll know what this is about?"

"It's really about my son, Lucas, Luke Magrady," he said evenly. "My number is on the back."

"Okay," she said, not promising anything. But she put the shot aside and not under the counter.

A little more than two hours later, Kang Fu called Magrady on his cell.

"You claim to have the shaman's head?" the unhurried voice asked.

"I do," he answered. "In exchange for getting me to my son, I'll negotiate a price for it."

"You're going about that all wrong, aren't you, hombre? Isn't it the head in exchange for your son?"

"I'm pretty certain he hasn't been kidnapped," Magrady said. "Just hard to find."

"For you."

"Precisely."

There was silence, then, "Well then," and he hung up.

Nothing to do but wait. Magrady bought two pre-packaged portobella mushroom sandwiches and some juice at a D'Agostino supermarket. He ate them in his prison cell of a room at a hotel on East 44th that Bonilla had found for him on the cheap via one of those internet specials. He was laying on the bed, watching CNN when he got the return call.

"The Aparo Club. Tonight, after ten. A car will be sent for you," a female voice said. Magrady told her where he was but he had a notion she might have already known that. The call over, he stood for a few moments at the window, arms folded, trying to decipher just what his son was involved in and how deep.

He chuckled dryly. He recalled several times cajoling his then teenaged son to help him balance the books when he had the distribution business. How the hell would he possibly know what Luke was up to given it involved high finance and who knows what else now? Magrady barely knew his multiplication tables and that was fast eluding him. Luke was now, thirty-one, no, thirty-two. He was a grown man and was, he hoped, capable of falling down the rabbit hole and climbing back out on his own.

Still, a man's son is a man's son. He showered, shaved, and put on the sport coat he'd brought with him, purchased at the Goodwill store in Culver City.

The car that came for him was a customary black Navigator. Wes Montgomery on the sound system, and eschewing the scotch offered by the female driver, they rode languidly over the bridge. The vehicle arrived at the Brooklyn Navy Yard, a development on the waterfront signage informed Magrady. They parked near an unmarked building and the driver opened the rear door for him.

Dressed in the male fantasy chauffeur's outfit of tight, short skirt and double-breasted tunic complete with the requisite cap, the copper-hued driver with the dynamite legs escorted him to a metal door.

"Enjoy," she said and returned to her vehicle.

He looked after her and back to the door, which slid open quietly. He entered an elevator car and rode up several stories and was let out on a vestibule furnished in antique wares, all polished wood and plush rococo chairs. There were blue velvet curtained archways on either side of the vestibule.

A statuesque bronze blonde woman in a tiger skin breechcloth and little else entered from the right and took his hand. "This way," she said, and led him through the curtain on the left. Magrady entered an area where he expected all manner of debauchery to be taking place. There were some goings on, but understated. He saw two men dressed in superhero costumes playing chess, several women in business attire or stylish underwear sitting on pillows sharing a hookah, each with violet hair cut in radical hairstyles, and a knot of nude men and women dancing. He didn't hear any music, but each of the dancers had a single wireless ear bud. He could smell marijuana but didn't see anybody toking up.

They went up a short flight of stairs and he was deposited in a small upholstered alcove.

"How do you wish to partake?" the blonde asked neutrally, cocking her head and smiling.

"Lemonade or juice is just fine," he said.

"That's all?" She stepped into his space, not breaking eye contact.

"Yes," he said reluctantly. The blonde was making him damn uncomfortable. He felt he could have asked for a bj and she would have obliged. Damn Kang Fu and his tests.

Magrady sat while techno music emanated softly from hidden speakers. His lemonade arrived and he sipped and grooved along with a remix of more Wes Montgomery, this time on his rendition of "Eleanor Rigby." Soon he was dozing.

"Hey, Dad," his son said and he opened his eyes.

"Luke," Magrady said getting up and hugging him.

"Good to see you too," the younger man said, patting his father's back as they separated. He was two inches taller than his father, lean as he remembered him, and favoring his mother in his facial features. His hair was cropped bald short as was the modern style, and a small gold hoop earring hung from his left lobe.

"You've lost some weight," Luke Magrady said, sitting down. He was dressed in dark slacks and a ribbed sweater-shirt that highlighted his athletic frame. "And who you been boxing?" He pointed at his father's bandaged ear.

"Long story."

"We got time."

They sat and Magrady told him about Floyd Chambers, his sister, Nakano, and Talmock's mummified head. He also told him he'd returned the head though he joked he'd been tempted to keep it as a paperweight.

"Damn," his son said appreciatively.

Magrady sat forward. "Look, I came because me and your sister are worried about you. Also, your mother—"

"I know about Mom." He sliced the air with a hand. "That's covered."

"Okay, but what about you? I know it's been hit or miss with me as your old man, but I can help. I want to help."

"There's nothing to help with, Pop. Everything's under control."

He shook a finger at him. "I used to say that right before I'd go off on a binge."

Luke Magrady laughed warmly and touched his father on the shoulder and squeezed. "You're getting by on that crap disability check? You don't have to, you know."

"Your boy Kang Fu gonna break me off something?"

He sat back, tenting his fingers. "It's complicated."

"But you could go to jail."

"For what?"

"For whatever bullshit you're mixed up in, Luke."

"You see the cops come busting in here? I look like I'm not getting my winks?"

Magrady shook his head. "I didn't come to argue."

"Neither did I."

"I just hope you know what you're doing."

"What do you think I'm doing, Em?"

It bugged him when his children called him by his nickname. "Some kind of credit default swap Wall Street Lehman Brothers hocus pocus."

"I assure you, what I'm doing is . . . kosher."

"Said the rabbi before he bit into his pork chop sandwich."

"You want one? I know you ain't converted to the crescent and the star." Luke smiled devilishly.

One slip was okay. "Sure. Got some potato salad to go with that?"

"No doubt, and greens too."

The two enjoyed their meal of pork chop sandwiches done fancy with the broiled meat having been rubbed in chili powder and some savory herb Magrady couldn't identify. This between thick slices of toasted sourdough bread with tomatoes and grilled onions. He shouldn't have been greedy in front of his son, but it took little encouragement for him to have a second one. He did, but ate it slower this time.

While they ate, their talk revolved on sports, world politics and their never-ending comic book debates on all things comic books.

"Really, you're telling me Gil Kane's run on Green Lantern stands the test of time and Kirby's '60s Captain America doesn't?" the father incredulously asked the son, his sandwich partway to his mouth.

Luke Magrady spread his arms wide. "Come on, Pop. Kirby and his clunky anatomy have been way overrated. Kane was all about grace and composition."

"Pretty poses that's all," the elder Magrady said, swallowing, and drinking more lemonade. "Kirby was about the action, just one of his drawings of someone dialing the phone was dynamic."

"That's 'cause he was too damn dramatic," his son quipped, having some of his beer.

"Next you're gonna tell me Mike Esposito was a regular Neal Adams."

"He had his strengths."

"Sheeet."

His son laughed. When Magrady had come home from Vietnam he'd brought back some comic books that had been sent over to the GIs by the various companies, mostly DCs and Marvels and a few like the Jaguar and the Fly from the company that published Archie. For a while he kept collecting them as reading those stories, and digging on the art of Kane, Kirby, Wally Wood, Marie Severin drawing the Sub-Mariner, and the others, was four-color therapy. The stories of flawed good against titanic evil, and what with being able to read what was on people's minds, via the thought balloons, that was comforting.

Even their foibles spoke to him. Like Daredevil being torn between the Black Widow and Karen Page in his love life.. Magrady had reasoned then, what man in his right cotton-picking mind wouldn't be all over that fine-ass widow? Still, those comics made a kind of sense he couldn't quite sync up to the real world. Those stories helped him ease back to the world.

So when Luke was born and began reading, and the older Esther wasn't much into these boys' adventures, he'd given his trove to his son. Luke Magrady bought and traded comics until fifteen or so, then switched his energies toward girls and basketball.

Magrady stretched and sank back into the upholstery. "That was great, Luke. All of it." His eyes misted up and he coughed to cover his wiping them.

His son touched him on the knee. "Sorry we can't hang out more, but some of the sorts I deal with are getting into their offices now." It was two in the morning. "I've got you a suite at the Plaza, not the hovel you've been staying in."

The father was on his feet. "Thanks, Kang Fu."

His son looked up at him, squinting with one eye. "When did you know?"

"Not right off, though the name did nag at me. And having somebody else be you on the phone threw me of course. But when we were talking about the comics artists it flipped on that Kang Fu was one of the mystic elders who advised Lionhead Mose, your superhero, in that story you wrote and drew."

His son was also standing, smiling broadly. "Good to see that booze and dope didn't destroy all your damn grey matter."

The two walked out to the front of the club, the navigator waiting for Magrady. The elbow Wakefield Nakano had smashed with his mallet ached in the cold.

"Call your sister, will you?" Magrady said as he gingerly massaged his tender elbow.

"Okay, Pop."

They hugged each other tight. Magrady stayed for three days and nights at the Plaza, enjoyed room service, saw the city, and talked to Luke over the phone, though didn't see him in person again. He flew back home in first class for his first time thanks to his generous son—a son he hoped wasn't heading to the hoosegow.

Back in L.A., he started work as a community organizer for Urban Advocacy.

"BUT I'M GONNA PUT A CAT ON YOU"
GARY PHILLIPS INTERVIEWED BY DENISE HAMILTON

How'd The Underbelly *come about?*

The Underbelly was initially written as an online serial a couple of years ago for the fourstory.org site because Nathan Walpow, a fellow mystery writer, asked me if I wanted to contribute to the site. Because Nathan had a background in fiction, he was also looking to add to the site, to augment the nonfiction with fiction, to broaden the site. Not just dry pieces about housing and homelessness. In fact nowadays the site runs stories about issues like housing, sustainable living and transportation, riffs on pop culture, to other fiction and even pieces on Cuba based on a trip the FourStory staff took to the island nation not too long ago. So, really, honestly, they're not dry pieces.

Anyway, Nathan knew I had a background as a community organizer and that my wife was an urban planner and ran a nonprofit. I drew on those experiences to write the novella. Essentially, the plot centers on a semi-homeless Vietnam vet named Magrady who's now been sober for eight months. He was on and off booze and drugs for years and suffers from flashbacks. A disabled friend of his, a man in a wheelchair, who's not a vet, but lives on Skid Row, disappears, and Magrady has to find him. This sets the plot in motion.

The story takes place in Los Angeles, and that was the point of locating it in the sphere of FourStory, which is to say it takes place in a gentrifying downtown Los Angeles. And à la L.A. Live, this complex of venues recently built there that includes the Staples Center where the pro-basketball Lakers play and nightclubs, restaurants, and a large hotel, there's a mega development project in the book called the Emerald Shoals. This project like in real life has displaced working poor folks and impacted the homeless as the so-called urban pioneers move into converted lofts and the like. To reflect this one of the characters in the book is a community organizer named Janis Bonilla who is a friend of Magrady's and also an organizer for a community empowerment organization.

Hopefully *Underbelly* walks the line between having substantive issues as context, helping to ground a story, and being on a soapbox with just having the story as an excuse for a polemic.

Is it bad literature to write polemic stories?

If I want a polemic I'll read nonfiction. As storytellers, it's our job not to be the opiate of the masses but if you're going to tell a story, it should have characters that resonate with the reader and have a plot and structure and is just not an excuse to go on forever.

Take for example John D. MacDonald, a mystery writer who created the Travis McGee character and series. It seems to me he got consumed at the end of his writing career with his own conservative politics, and there would be long passages in his books having his characters ranting on about environmentalists, treehuggers, and lefties, but the job of the writer or storyteller is to tell a story. Obviously you want to have these realities in your work but you have to be clever about weaving that stuff in your story.

I think peoples' points of view certainly come into play, so that's fine, but I'm also interested in having characters having different points of view. It makes for better drama, right? Characters always want something, and invariably these interests collide.

Another example is a book of mine called *Freedom's Fight*. The novel is about African American soldiers and civilians during World War II. In the book we see the racism and conflicts the all-black units encounter with white soldiers. Because of Jim Crow policies, black troops weren't sent into combat until end of 1943, beginning of 1944. The story also unfolds through the eyes of a black woman reporter, Alma Yates, for the *Pittsburgh Courier*, the largest black weekly newspaper at the time.

Via her, the reader gets glimpses of what's happening in the States. The *Courier* was part of something called the Double V Campaign, victory at home and victory overseas. During that time there were arguments among civil rights organization and on the left about the role of the black soldier. Why should they fight and die for freedom abroad if they didn't have freedom here at home, versus the pressure for African Americans to show white America they were good, loyal citizens.

Freedom's Fight came about as my way to tell a slice of this bigger story. I think I'm accurate in stating there are less than a handful of novels about black soldiers during this period—though certainly there are several informative nonfiction books such as *The Invisible Soldier* by Mary Penick Molley, *Lasting Valor* by Medal of Honor winner Vern Baker and Ken Olsen, and *Brothers in Arms* about the 761st tank battalion by Kareem Abdul-Jabbar and Anthony Walton.

But if you watched the TV miniseries *Brothers in Arms* or now the recent *Pacific* on cable, you wouldn't have any idea that there were all-black units who fought in those theaters of conflict, but there were. My late dad Dikes was in combat at Guadalcanal, his brother, Norman, was at D-Day Plus One, and the youngest brother, Sammy, served in India. My mother, Leonelle, had a brother named Oscar Hutton Jr., who was shot down and killed over Memmingen, Germany, as a Tuskegee fighter pilot.

Given all that, I tried not to make *Freedom's Fight* preachy, but, hopefully, entertaining historical fiction with a socio-political grounding, and even some hardboiled elements—there is a murder mystery subplot, dimensional characters and action on the battlefield.

Speaking of which, when did noir get a grip on you?

I stumbled into it at as a kid, I played sports as a kid in school, but because my mom was a librarian, I was literally forced to read. When I came home from grade school I'd have to read

Pinocchio and Grimms' Fairy Tales for an hour before I could go out and play. I initially rebelled against this, but damned if I didn't come to like reading. And there's some pretty rugged stuff in those Grimm stories, including cannibalism and murder.

I still remember at 61st Street Elementary, they taught us the Dewey Decimal System, and I went to the school library and plucked off the shelf *20,000 Leagues Under the Sea* by Jules Verne and I was eight or nine, I hadn't even seen the Disney movie of the book so I don't know how I knew about it, but somehow I knew who Verne was.

How does that get us to noir? I started to develop a love of reading. Somewhere in this I was reading a lot of pulp stories because Bantam was reprinting Doc Savage and The Shadow. At this time I'm starting to watch mystery and detective stories on TV and I heard about Dashiell Hammett so I picked up some Hammett and read some of his short stories. It would be awhile before I read his Sam Spade novel the *Maltese Falcon*. But Hammett got me hooked, I liked the way he wrote, I liked his patter, and I liked that he wrote these tough, and in many ways, unsentimental stories, and from there I branched into Ross Macdonald, though that was a little later.

Then in 1970 when I'm still in high school, playing at the Temple Theater in my neighborhood in South Central was this movie called *Cotton Comes to Harlem*. I didn't know then about Chester Himes—the movie is based on his book of the same title—but the film looked cool what with two black actors dressing '70s-slick in the lead roles as Harlem cops. The stars were comedian Godfrey Cambridge as Gravedigger Jones and Raymond St. Jacques as Coffin Ed Johnson, with Redd Foxx in a supporting role as, yes, a junk man—this before his fame as Fred Sanford on the TV show *Sanford and Son*. Foxx I knew from his ribald party records—and I'm talking vinyl LPs, long play, here—my dad would play for his friends when they came over for beers. Naturally I was sent off to bed but always managed to hear some of Foxx's dirty jokes through my slightly cracked door.

This early '70s is the beginning of the blaxploitation cycle of movies Hollywood ground out, a lot of them with mystery and crime plots. Seeing *Cotton* gets me to Himes. At some point I began reading his work, a blend of oddball characters, crazy plots and rumination on race relations in America. What always struck me about noir and hard boiled stories is one I enjoyed them because they were crime stories, walks on the wild side . . . and two, they always looked at what exists in the shadows, the flip side of human personalities. Plus they're great morality tales.

But sometimes the bad guy wins. What kind of morality is that?

Maybe that's the hard truth, the real truth that life teaches us. When there are ambiguous endings or the bad guy wins. Thus the metaphor for capitalism, I suppose. The character in the novel out to take down the bank or knock over the racetrack is the stripped-down robber baron with no pretense at anything else than being a gangster capitalist. Could be noir is a trap of the proletariat. Your character thinks he or she can change their station in life if only they can get away with this crime . . . but they're sucked down. Though this can happen to well-off characters. Hell, sometimes the working class gets the upper hand in noir. But only sometimes.

Recently too I saw read this mention of a nonfiction book entitled *American Homicide* by a historian named Randolph Roth. Roth posits that high homicide rates "are not determined by proximate causes such as poverty, drugs, unemployment, alcohol, race, or ethnicity, but by factors . . . like the feelings that people have toward their government and the opportunities they have to earn respect without resorting to violence." Roth also stated that looking at FBI stats from the first six months in 2009 taken from the urban areas Obama carried in his election for the presidency, saw the steepest drop in the homicide rate since the mid-nineties.

Of course you also have a rise in neofascist racist groups, and I include the teabaggers in this mix, as a result of Obama's presidency, so there's that. But it does suggest there can be further interesting takes on noir if you track Roth's theories.

How'd you cross the bridge from reader to writer?

In my twenties, because I was involved in community activist work, anti-apartheid and police abuse organizing and the like, and because I had a bent for art in those days, but that was only because I wanted to draw and write comic books. This meant I'd wind up being on the committees to write and design the flyers for a march or a demonstration. Fact for a while in the mid- to late '80s, I was the co-owner of a print shop in South Central we'd started from the funds my comrade the late Michael Zinzun had put up. He was one of the founders of the Coalition Against Police Abuse, CAPA, and had won a suit after being beaten by the Pasadena Police Department and losing an eye. Our shop, a union shop, I might add, was called 42nd Street Litho and we'd print pamphlets, newsletters, and flyers and I was always involved with writing some of those given the various organizations I was involved in as well. But like Raymond Chandler, I didn't start 'til I was in my thirties writing fiction. By then I figured out what I wanted to do was write a book.

Specifically I'd been fired from a union organizing job in 1989. I'd been working for the American Federation of State, County and Municipal Employees, AFSCME, and this particular local, Council 10, represented the groundskeepers and some of the library personnel at UCLA, the university here in Los Angeles. Having time on my hands and talking it over with my wife Gilda, I decided to take this extension class being taught at the university about writing your mystery novel. The class was taught by Bob Crais, who then was coming out of TV as a script writer on shows like *Hill Street Blues* and *Cagney & Lacey*, and had turned to writing mystery novels.

In Bob's class we deconstructed the first Spenser novel by Robert Parker, the *Godwulf Manuscript,* about this illuminated artifact being stolen. We then had to come up with an outline and the first fifty pages of our own novels. It's there that I came up with my private eye character Ivan Monk and the people in his world. The class was over in, I think, ten weeks, but I went on and finished that first book. I didn't get it published but was happy to have just written it.

I guess I always knew I'd write a mystery novel because that's what I'd been reading, all kinds of people from the established pantheon—Chandler, Hammett, and Macdonald— even Dorothy L. Sayers and her Lord Peter Wimsey stories, to black writers like Donald Goines and Iceberg Slim, Robert Beck. Iceberg, from whom rapper-actor Ice-T derived his stage moniker, had been a pimp and consorted with all types of low life individuals back east. He retired from the "Life," and came west. He drew on those harsh experiences to craft his street level fiction for paperback originals for the white-owned Holloway House here in L.A.

Goines, a former Air Force military policeman (he enlisted underage, using a fake birth certificate), rooty-poot pimp, petty thief, heroin addict, truck driver and hustler, among his other pursuits, wrote sixteen paperback originals for Holloway House, starting with *Dopefiend*, published in late 1971. His writing routine was grind out pages in the morning and go score dope in the afternoon. His last two books would be released posthumously in 1975. One was *Kenyatta's Last Hit*, a series he wrote about this politicized gangster, and attributed to him, *Inner City Hoodlum*.

But as Eddie Allen relates in his biography about Goines, *Low Road*, *Inner City Hoodlum*'s parentage was not Goines' solely, but also that of a writer named Carleton Hollander. Allen states Hollander had to heavily edit and finish the uncompleted manuscript that Goines had left behind. I also know from my friend Emory Holmes, who was an editor two different times at Holloway House, that Goines' use of heroin often impaired his page outage.

You see, Mr. Goines exited this world in as violent a fashion as any depicted in his books. He and Shirley Sailor, who lived together and had two children, were shot to death in their apartment at 232 Cortland in Detroit, their bodies found on the morning of October 22, 1974. Fortunately, the murderers hadn't harmed the children. Like some Ross Macdonald mystery embedded in the past but reverberating to the present day, the killers remain unidentified.

So in those days you'd find Goines' books and Iceberg Slim's in my neighborhood in South Central at the Thrifty's, the CVS drug store of its day. You wouldn't find them at the B Dalton and the Pickwick bookstores. Now you can find their stuff at the chains. These two cats, for good and ill, are considered the godfathers of what's called Ghetto Lit now.

Circling back to the *Godwulf Manuscript*, and apropos of the kind of stories Goines and Beck wrote, what I remember in that book is Spenser beds a mother and subsequently her grown daughter in the course of the story, because he was that kind of stud. Maybe that was the lesson we were supposed to learn about PI characters.

Well, after writing my first book, I knew I had to write another book. After the L.A. riots or the civil unrest, depending on your political point of view, in 1992, at that time I was working at a nonprofit, the Liberty Hill Foundation. Then and still today, they grant money to community organizing. So I knew a lot of the players in L.A., the mainstream local power brokers as well as grassroots people and some of the ones involved in the gang truce. Knowing this range of folks, I thought I could then write a mystery novel set after the riots—a mystery set amid a changing racial and political landscape. It was titled *Violent Spring*, with my PI Ivan Monk delving into the death of a Korean merchant in South Central. The book eventually got published, despite some publishers telling me in their rejection letters to drop the socio-political aspects of the novel. The book even got optioned for HBO and I did the Hollywood shuffle. Hilarious.

But now I was hooked. I'd written one book, I had to write the next one. 'Cause you're only as good as the last book . . . your last trick. Which gets us to today, twelve or so novels later and some short stories, anthologies and scripts I've banged out, the deal is to keep repeating the trick, which is especially arduous given the state of publishing today. Or maybe it's easier, because you don't have to worry about a publisher buying your next book. Anyway, maybe it's a good thing you won't need to publish your book in the traditional way. It's gotten harder and harder to sell a book given it's all about the P & L—the profit and loss on your last book.

Is that because of e-publishing and the Kindle?

Yeah, because with the Kindle, iPad, and what have you, and just to bite the hand that feeds, why do we need publishers, if there's no real book, no physical copy? So what is the publisher's role if they're not "publishing" a hard copy of the book? We now have some cases of young writers like my boy Seth Harwood, who wrote *Jack Wakes Up* and *Young Junius*, who have gone this route. Initially they publish an e-book, even doing podcasts of reading the chapters. They then work the social media, Facebooking and twittering and who knows what else, building up an audience. So they can quantify a readership based on downloads and hits, and counterintuitively, the same people who got the book for free or cheap electronically, a good number of those folks, went out and bought their books when these works came out as real books. I mean, a book you can feel and smell, man.

It seems to me then that there is still an attachment by some people to the book as an artifact. They want a hard copy sitting on their shelf. Will this be the case with the new generation?

I don't think so. I hope so, but young people growing up in a paperless society won't need or want the hard copy of the book. For them a book isn't an artifact. Conversely, there are still books that catch fire. There seems to be young people, among other people, who will go out and buy those books.

What I'm curious about is what is the demographic breakdown of those who are buying hard copy books vs e-books. I would bet it's heavily young people.

My wife Gilda recently read a book on her iPhone, *The Devil in the White City* by Erik Larson. And because she was engaged in the story, she didn't care that she was reading it on this little device, though she showed it to me on the iPhone and the text was pretty readable. The fact remains we still need and want stories. There will always be a need and a hunger for stories. That's just how our brains are hardwired. I guess something about order in the chaos that's life. And we're storytellers, whatever form that takes. Someone still has to come up with the plot, the characters and situations. But it seems to be the case now that when the publisher takes on your book, they expect you to quantify and deliver your audience.

I try not to think too hard about the future of publishing. If I did that I'd never write another book. I just keep telling my stories and being optimistic that it will still find an audience.

I agree.

What's your muse?

Deadlines. Seriously, I'm reluctant to say that I have a muse because to me, as a commercial writer, a genre writer, I write better if I have a deadline. The pressure. If I had any muse, it would be the ghosts of my mom the librarian and my dad the mechanic who always encouraged me, particularly about writing. Especially my dad, Dikes, because he didn't have much of an education, he had to drop out of school in the sixth grade. I grew up hearing his stories. He was born in 1912, so was a teenager and grown man during the Great Depression. He dug ditches making highways for the Works Progress Administration, was a lookout as a kid for a bootlegger in his hometown of Seguin, Texas, was an iceman delivering blocks of ice to cold water flats in Chicago, delivered bodies to the mortuary, chopped cotton for a quarter for a day's work, and so on.

Eventually his older brother Norman came out to L.A. and got a job and had Pop come out too. I grew up hearing his stories, of being a young man on Central Avenue, the jazz clubs and night spots then as given the segregation of L.A., blacks were on the East Side of the city and Central Avenue became the Stem, it was called, of black life. Hotels, doctors, dentists, newspapers like the *Eagle* and the *Sentinel*, they were there on or around Central Avenue. He got drafted, going to the war . . . I grew up hearing those stories, and those are the tales that stuck with me then and even today.

Los Angeles itself is certainly an inspiration and a continuing character for me. I think L.A. can be plumbed for a lot of ideas. As thin as the *L.A. Times* is now, there's always something you read in the paper, see on the news, hear somewhere that invariably sparks an idea in me. I carry that around with me and make little notes. At some point it worries your brain enough that you have to write the story.

I'm also fascinated with the retelling of tales often told. How many versions of timeless iconic characters like Frankenstein, Sherlock Holmes, and Robin Hood are there . . . yet there always seem to be room for more—allowing for different angles and perspectives on the characters. Or take the late comedian, the monologist Lord Buckley, Richard Buckley. This big, six-foot-six onetime lumberjack white guy from the sticks in upper California, who reinvents himself as a bebop hipster with a baritone voice, a pith helmet, and Salvador Dalí-type moustache doing a aristocratic English accent knocking it back with black slang.

"But I'm gonna put a cat on you who was the coolest, grooviest, sweetest, wailin'est strongest cat that ever stomped on this sweet, swingin' sphere. And they called this here cat, the Nazz."

This is part of Buckley's version of the life of Jesus of Nazareth. Cool and crazy. See, it's all in the telling.

Someone, I forget who, said, you will write when it hurts more not to write. Agree?

(Nods) Plus writing is such good therapy. I don't know what I'd do if I couldn't write.

And L.A. is such a rich cauldron to draw from: various classes, races, cultures, undocumented immigration . . .

Absolutely.

They're not going to stop coming. Until we help stabilize Mexico's economy, stop selling them guns and genetically modified corn. No border can stop it. We are all part of a continuum.

That's right. Our job is to go out and get those stories and tell them.

What's noir then?

Looking at this book you have here on your table about William Mulholland, who engineered the bringing of water, or some would argue helped steal that water, to make what has become the modern metropolis of Los Angeles, drives home the concept of L.A. as the seat or crucible of noir. Even though the word 'noir' is bandied about a lot these days, to me the term refers to a doomed character or characters consumed or at least driven by lust, greed, gluttony, revenge . . . one of those baser instincts of us humans.

Invariably this bent mental state gets the character all caught up; when they should turn left they turn right, when they should keep walking, they turn the knob on that battered door and their fate can only spiral down into the velvet whirlpool. Noir means doomed characters in search of a doomed destiny, but they don't know this and they can't help themselves. They're self-deluded but they're making themselves self deluded by lust or greed. Usually it's one of the seven deadly sins but there are only two or three of those that really trip people up. Ha.

They can't see up for down, wrong for right, because they want something. It's usually not a big thing. It's a reasonable thing. They want money but they don't want a lot of money. A couple hundred thousand, let's say. Or you desire your neighbor's wife 'cause she looks so damn good in that summer dress.

So noir is personal?

It's your own undoing that you if not willingly, at least subconsciously, participate in and bring about. When you should make a left turn, you make a right. When you should lock that door, you open it. Because you're driven, obsessed. Often it's a situation you've put yourself in. Noir will kill ya.

Denise Hamilton writes crime fiction set in contemporary, multicultural Los Angeles. Her novels have been short-listed for every major mystery award. She is also the editor of the Edgar Award winning short story anthology *Los Angeles Noir* (that Phillips has a story in) and *Los Angeles Noir 2: the Classics*. Visit her at www.denisehamilton.com.

BIBLIOGRAPHY

The Underbelly (2010)
The Jook (1999, and PM Press, 2009)
The Perpetrators (2002)
Bangers (2003)
*Freedom's Fight (*2009*)*
Kings of Vice (2010)

Ivan Monk Series
Violent Spring (1994)
Perdition, U.S.A. (1995)
Bad Night Is Falling (1998)
Only the Wicked (2000)
Monkology: 13 Stories From the World of Private Eye Ivan Monk
(2004)

Martha Chainey Series
High Hand (2000)
Shooter's Point (2001)

Short Stories
"King Cow" & "Hollywood Killer," *Angeltown: The Nate Hollis Investigations* (2010)
"The Investor," *Damn Near Dead 2* (2010)
"The Performer," *Orange County Noir* (2010)
"The Snow Birds" *Once Upon a Crime* (2009)
"Blazin' on Broadway," *Phoenix Noir* (2009)
"The Thrill is Gone," *Sex, Lies and Private Eyes* (2009)
"The New Me," *Noir: A Collection of Crime Comics* (2009)
"House of Tears," *Black Noir: Mystery, Crime, and Suspense Stories by African-American Writers* (2009). Originally ran in the first issue of *Murdaland*.

"Swift Boats for Jesus," *Politics Noir* (2008)

"The Freeze Devil," *The Avenger Chronicles* (2008)

"The Kim Novak Effect," *Ellery Queen Mystery Magazine* (2008). Reprinted in *Between the Dark and the Daylight.*

"And What Shall We Call You?" *The Darker Mask: Heroes from the Shadows* (2008)

"Roger Crumbler Considered His Shave," *Los Angeles Noir,* (2007)

"Where All Our Dreams Come True," *Hollywood and Crime: Original Crime Stories Set During the History of Hollywood* (2007)

"Sportin' Men," *Full House,* (2007)

"The Man For the Job," *Dublin Noir: The Celtic Tiger vs. The Ugly American* (2006)

"Blues, Sex, and Bad Hot Mojo" & "Broken Willow," *Kolchak: The Night Stalker Casebook* (2006)

"Incident on Hill 19," *Retro Pulp Tales* (2006)

"The Socratic Method," amazon.com shorts (2006)

"Disco Zombies," *Cocaine Chronicles* (2005)

"Searching for Cisa," *Kolchak: The Night Stalker Chronicles* (2005)

"Chatter," *Plots With Guns: A Noir Anthology* (2005)

"The Accomplice," *Creature Cozies* (2005)

"Beginner's Luck," *Shades of Black: Crime and Mystery Stories by African-American Writers* (2004)

"Branded," *Flesh & Blood: Erotic Tales of Crime and Passion* (2003)

"Rio Blanco," *Guns of the West,* (2002)

"Hollywood Spring and Axle," *The Mighty Johns and Other Stories* (2002)

"The Counterfeit Comrade," *Measures of Poison* (2002)

"The Measure," *The Blue and the Grey Undercover: All New Civil War Spy Adventures* (2001)

As editor or coeditor:
The Cocaine Chronicles (2005)
Politics Noir (2008)
The Darker Mask (2008)
Orange County Noir (2010)

ABOUT THE AUTHOR

Influenced by the likes of writer Rod Serling, comic book artists Jack Kirby and Jim Steranko, the records of comedians Bill Cosby and Richard Pryor, enchanted when Shirley Bassey sang "Goldfinger," and never forgetting those stories his father told of being on the road during the Great Depression, what else could Gary Phillips do but make stuff up? He currently writes a darkly funny webcomic, *Bicycle Cop Dave,* on www.fourstory. org, ghostwrote an upcoming crime novel with pioneer rapper-actor Ice-T, writes the further adventures of pulp spy character Operator 5 for Moonstone Comics, and has a crime graphic novel forthcoming from DC/Vertigo Comics entitled *Cowboys*.

GARY PHILLIPS

The Jook
978-1-60486-0405
$15.95

Zelmont Raines has slid a long way since his ability to jook, to out maneuver his opponents on the field, made him a Super Bowl–winning wide receiver, earning him lucrative endorsement deals and more than his share of female attention. But Zee hasn't always been good at saying no, so a series of missteps involving drugs, a paternity suit or two, legal entanglements, shaky investments, and recurring injuries have virtually sidelined his career.

That is until Los Angeles gets a new pro franchise, the Barons, and Zelmont has one last chance at the big time he dearly misses. Just as it seems he might be getting back in the flow, he's enraptured by Wilma Wells, the leggy and brainy lawyer for the team—who has a ruthless game plan all her own. And it's Zelmont who might get jooked.

Praise:
"Phillips, author of the acclaimed Ivan Monk series, takes elements of Jim Thompson (the ending), black-exploitation flicks (the profanity-fueled dialogue), and *Penthouse* magazine (the sex is anatomically correct) to create an over-the-top violent caper in which there is no honor, no respect, no love, and plenty of money. Anyone who liked George Pelecanos' King Suckerman is going to love this even-grittier take on many of the same themes."
—Wes Lukowsky, *Booklist*

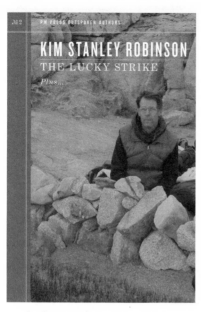

PM PRESS
OUTSPOKEN AUTHORS

The Lucky Strike
Kim Stanley Robinson
978-1-60486-085-6
$12

Combining dazzling spec-
ulation with a profoundly
humanist vision, Kim Stanley Robinson is known as
not only the most literary
but also the most progres-
sive (read "radical") of today's top-rank SF authors.
His bestselling "Mars Tril-
ogy" tells the epic story of
the future colonization of the red planet, and the revolution that
inevitably follows. His latest novel, *Galileo's Dream*, is a stunning
combination of historical drama and far-flung space opera, in
which the ten dimensions of the universe itself are rewoven to
ensnare history's most notorious torturers.

The Lucky Strike, the classic and controversial story Robinson
has chosen for PM's new Outspoken Authors series, begins on
a lonely Pacific island, where a crew of untested men are about
to take off in an untried aircraft with a deadly payload that will
change our world forever. Until something goes wonderfully
wrong.

Plus: *A Sensitive Dependence on Initial Conditions*, in which Robinson dramatically deconstructs "alternate history" to explore
what might have been if things had gone differently over Hiro-
shima that day.

As with all Outspoken Author books, there is a deep interview
and autobiography: at length, in-depth, no-holds-barred and all-
bets off: an extended tour though the mind and work, the history
and politics of our Outspoken Author. Surprises are promised.

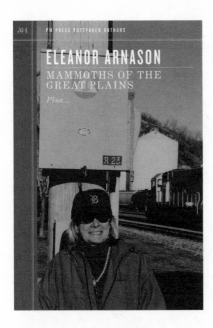

PM PRESS
OUTSPOKEN AUTHORS

Mammoths of the Great Plains
Eleanor Arnason
978-1-60486-075-7
$12

When President Thomas Jefferson sent Lewis and Clark to explore the West, he told them to look especially for mammoths. Jefferson had seen bones and tusks of the great beasts in Virginia, and he suspected—he hoped!—that they might still roam the Great Plains. In Eleanor Arnason's imaginative alternate history, they do: shaggy herds thunder over the grasslands, living symbols of the oncoming struggle between the Native peoples and the European invaders. And in an unforgettable saga that soars from the badlands of the Dakotas to the icy wastes of Siberia, from the Russian Revolution to the AIM protests of the 1960s, Arnason tells of a modern woman's struggle to use the weapons of DNA science to fulfill the ancient promises of her Lakota heritage.

PLUS: "Writing SF During World War III," and an Outspoken Interview that takes you straight into the heart and mind of one of today's edgiest and most uncompromising speculative authors.

Praise:
"Eleanor Arnason nudges both human and natural history around so gently in this tale that you hardly know you're not in the world-as-we-know-it until you're quite at home in a North Dakota where you've never been before, listening to your grandmother tell you the world."   —Ursula K. Le Guin

FRIENDS OF

These are indisputably momentous times—the financial system is melting down globally and the Empire is stumbling. Now more than ever there is a vital need for radical ideas.

In the three years since its founding—and on a mere shoestring—PM Press has risen to the formidable challenge of publishing and distributing knowledge and entertainment for the struggles ahead. With over 100 releases to date, we have published an impressive and stimulating array of literature, art, music, politics, and culture. Using every available medium, we've succeeded in connecting those hungry for ideas and information to those putting them into practice.

Friends of PM allows you to directly help impact, amplify, and revitalize the discourse and actions of radical writers, filmmakers, and artists. It provides us with a stable foundation from which we can build upon our early successes and provides a much-needed subsidy for the materials that can't necessarily pay their own way. You can help make that happen – and receive every new title automatically delivered to your door once a month – by joining as a Friend of PM Press. And, we'll throw in a free T-Shirt when you sign up.

Here are your options:

• $25 a month: Get all books and pamphlets plus 50% discount on all webstore purchases.

• $25 a month: Get all CDs and DVDs plus 50% discount on all webstore purchases.

• $40 a month: Get all PM Press releases plus 50% discount on all webstore purchases

• $100 a month: Sustainer. - Everything plus PM merchandise, free downloads, and 50% discount on all webstore purchases.

For those who can't afford $25 or more a month, we're introducing Sustainer Rates at $15, $10 and $5. Sustainers get a free PM Press t-shirt and a 50% discount on all purchases from our website.

Just go to **WWW.PMPRESS.ORG** to sign up. Your Visa or Mastercard will be billed once a month, until you tell us to stop. Or until our efforts succeed in bringing the revolution around. Or the financial meltdown of Capital makes plastic redundant. Whichever comes first.financial meltdown of Capital makes plastic redundant. Whichever comes first.

PM PRESS was founded at the end of 2007 by a small collection of folks with decades of publishing, media, and organizing experience. PM Press co-conspirators have published and distributed hundreds of books, pamphlets, CDs, and DVDs. Members of PM have founded enduring book fairs, spearheaded victorious tenant organizing campaigns, and worked closely with bookstores, academic conferences, and even rock bands to deliver political and challenging ideas to all walks of life. We're old enough to know what we're doing and young enough to know what's at stake.

We seek to create radical and stimulating fiction and non-fiction books, pamphlets, t-shirts, visual and audio materials to entertain, educate and inspire you. We aim to distribute these through every available channel with every available technology - whether that means you are seeing anarchist classics at our bookfair stalls; reading our latest vegan cookbook at the café; downloading geeky fiction e-books; or digging new music and timely videos from our website.

PM Press is always on the lookout for talented and skilled volunteers, artists, activists and writers to work with. If you have a great idea for a project or can contribute in some way, please get in touch.

PM PRESS
PO Box 23912
Oakland CA 94623
510-658-3906
www.pmpress.org